NITARA

usa today bestselling author

JESSICA CAGE

AUTOGRAPH
PAGE

Contents

Dedication

To the readers who recently filled my heart with such joy. Growing
up I always wanted to see myself represented in the stories I loved.
I have been overwhelmed by the recent support and gratitude that
I have gotten for daring to represent characters of color in such a
bold way.
To that little girl out there, dripping in melanin and immersed in
the world of fantasy, you too can be a vampire, fairy, or a dragon,
... you can be it all!

Prologue

This section of your novel is considered outside the main plot story, but will always be closely related to it.

You might use a prologue to introduce a character or setting, or provide relevant background information for the main event to come.

Similar to an introduction, a prologue is typically placed in the main body content of a book, before the first chapter, and is therefore not technically front matter.

CHAPTER I

Welcome Home

"*My darling, Nitara finally came back to me.*" The voice of a narcissist dripping with ego echoed off the high ceilings and trilled in her ear. At least someone took pleasure in the moment of her return.

The sour faces of the other guests awaiting her told he was the only one. Not so shockingly. The lord of all who sucked was exactly where she expected to find him—ass sitting comfy in his gaudy throne, perched atop an elaborately accented, grand staircase. They framed the oversized seat in gold and silver; the same material lacing the banisters that reached down to her, an extension of the host, welcoming her home. At the top of the headrest was a large medallion stamped with an image of the letters 'V' and 'T'. V for Reverie, the city of vampires, and T for the tyrant that ruled it. Tyrellis.

"As if I really had any other choice?" She sneered as she passed his flunkies—vampires who looked as if they'd had way too much blood, which was likely laced with something much more toxic. This half-drugged state was the only way they could tolerate being around her without showing just how much her presence terrified them. Her arrival meant that the ego maniac at the top of the stairs was once again more powerful than any vampire had ever been.

"We both know there's always a choice." Tyrellis stood from his seat, and his wiry frame became lost beneath the heavy fabric of the gold cape draped over his shoulders. The only thing that could've made him look more ridiculous was if he'd added a crown.

He would have, if not for the urging of his wife to not adorn what she called a tacky accessory. In reality, he was no king. Blond hair fell in his eyes before he pushed the strands back into place, tucked tightly behind his ear. "Of course, making that choice would mean a lot of pain for you. I don't want you to be in any pain, Nitara." His concern for her was as shallow as his personality. If she didn't all but guarantee him the throne, he wouldn't give a damn about her being in pain.

"Oh, please spare me the dramatics, Tyrellis." Steps forced by magic carried her up the staircase and past more drugged out vampires who lay out on the gold trimmed steps.

2

Tyrellis' home was more of a gothic cathedral. Gaudy statues lined the main entrance with pillars that held up a high ceiling decorated in painted depictions of bloodlust. And that was only the entrance to a property that took up one hundred acres of prime land. Each wing, and there were many, had a different theme. Whenever the vampire leader got into another phase of his life, he would simply wish that she produce a space to commemorate it.

They covered the last addition in purple crushed velvet in honor of the human singer, Prince. Tyrellis had become nostalgic for a time that was centuries in the past. Playing at all hours were hits from the singer, and if anyone entered without dancing, they were to be flogged, a ridiculous rule that was rarely enforced, and not just because no one ever ventured into the space.

"Must everything be such a grand production with you?" Nitara rolled her eyes. "You called me. You knew I didn't want to be here, and yet here I am, because I have no other choice. Let's not pretend that this is a friendly visit, or my happy return to the blood den."

"Visit? Well, it's definitely not a visit, my Nitara. No, not this time. You've returned to me, and you're right where you belong. This time it's permanent, so no, I see no point in pretending otherwise." He paced the floor in small circles and kicked aside the half dazed women who lay at his feet. "Now that Daegal is gone, there's absolutely nothing that can take you away from me. You're mine now and forever!" He opened his arms to her

3

as she continued to ascend the steps against her will. "Come to me."

The final steps separating her reluctant body from his eager one disappeared beneath her feet, and she found herself in his arms, wrapped inside of the icy darkness that was his soulless body. She sighed, unwillingly welcoming the return of a punishment that she didn't deserve, and one that would never end. Daegal wanted to prove a point, and he'd done that. She wouldn't be with the love she desperately longed for ... instead, she would waste away as a djinn tied to a vampire by the darkest tethers of magic.

Nitara wished a life surrounded by bloodsuckers could be anything besides the stereotypical imaginings of most people. But it was exactly what one would expect. Once again, her life was a daily overflow of sex, bloodlust, and incessant whining. It wasn't just their egocentric personalities or their inability to lift a spoon to their lips without celebrating the act as if they'd invented the lightbulb. It was that nothing was ever good enough. Every ridiculous show was immediately reduced to mediocrity and replaced by one that was even more outlandish. And Nitara had the pleasure of being the one to make it all magically come to fruition!

The parameters of the post-apocalyptic world made it even more agreeable for the vampires to live their lives. No longer were they in hiding, the things that go bump in the night. When the unfortunate events revealed magic to the human world, none were more thrilled than the vampires. Quickly, they took over the night, terrifying the human population. That was until the fae stepped in. True beings of the night, the fae were determined to take it back. Though they were neutral in the war, they took on the battle with the vampires because the increase in their horrific acts were affecting the magic of the night. After a year of the vampires having free range to terrorize their prey, the stench of fear and evil clung to the air. The moment the sun escaped the sky, the world turned into a haunting place.

The moon fueled fae magic, so they were far more powerful when it shone, but the result of the rise in vampire activity stunted that connection. Vampires were beings made of a powerfully dark magic, quite like the djinn were. Whenever they were especially active, the collective pool of that magic seeped out into the world, tainting everything it touched. Still, they weren't strong enough to take on the fae. The outcome of the dispute between the two races was Reverie. The end of the brief battle resulted in vampires being given a defined territory where they could live their lives as freely as they wanted. This came with rules. If they got too out of hand, the fae were there to remind them. They put a head in place to regulate their activities and insure their continued survival. Tyrellis currently claimed that title.

No matter what wish Nitara granted for the vampires, it was never enough. After many failed attempts, she gave up all hope of trying to make any of them happy and learned that the best she could expect was that she could placate them long enough for her to get a decent night's sleep. Humans were much easier to please. She missed their simple requests. They wanted only enough to fulfill a single lifetime, not a thousand endless lives. With vampires, the wishes got more frivolous, and more ridiculous with time.

Her boots smacked against the hardwood floor of the bar as she monitored the tipsy population that was holed up inside. This was one of her duties, the vampire babysitter. She was Tyrellis' eyes and ears, which meant it was also her responsibility to keep the peace and make sure that none of the children did anything that would break the pact with the fae.

Though Nitara moved freely through the dark bar, no one acknowledged her presence. By design, the vamps only saw her when she wanted them to. The best watch dog was one that could go unnoticed. At the far end of the bar, sipping on a glass of thick, red liquid, was someone who'd unexpectantly become a regular at the bar. Frequently, she spotted him there, in the same position where he kept a close eye on the other vamps who patronized the establishment.

Unlike the others, he wasn't a member of the central nest that dwelled in the capital of Reverie. He was an outsider, one of those who refused to accept Tyrellis as their leader. If not for Nitara, his opposers would have challenged his position the moment he tried to take over. Instead, those who stood against him lived away from the principal cities. Most assumed they were plotting, trying to devise a way to get to Tyrellis.

It was because of these rumors Tyrellis often sent Nitara to the outskirts on recon missions. If any of the other rebels were to visit the local bar, her magic would have ripped them to pieces and returned their dismembered limbs back to the camps they came from. But not Graham. His reputation was one that allowed him access to areas which would otherwise be off limits to outsiders. It also helped that he was one of the oldest vampires around and most of the others didn't stand a chance against him in a fair fight. As far as Nitara could determine, the solo vampire posed no immediate threat to Tyrellis, so he was spared from her brutal judgment.

"You're back." The baritone voice of the dark-eyed man sitting at the end of the bar carried over the blues music that set the edgy yet relaxed tone to the bar's moody atmosphere. His tone still carried hints of the southern charm, though days of living in the southern state of Georgia were far behind him.

"Yeah," she huffed. Despite her magical cover, he could always sense her. She didn't know how.

Nitara dropped her barrier that kept her hidden from the others. And the place damn near cleared out. She ignored the hisses and gasps, and walked over to join him, claiming a stool for herself. She conjured up a drink of her own, something that didn't contain chromosomes from the local farmer.

"Couldn't stay away, huh?" He lifted his glass to hers and gave a toast to her return from the unknown.

"From this place? Never!" The sound of her glass punctuated her sarcastic response as it clinked against his before the hot shot of whisky traveled down her throat.

"Why do you hang around here?" He glanced over his shoulder where he eyed the scarce collection of drunkards who hadn't run from the sight of her. The overweight man in the corner belched, scratched his belly, and winked at him. "There has to be somewhere else a djinn like you would prefer to be."

"You always ask me that." She smiled. It was the same question every time they met. Graham was prying, but why?

She sucked her teeth as two women entered, giggling before they spotted her. With bucked eyes and descended fangs, they stopped in their tracks, and quickly turned to exit the bar. "How could I ever dream of missing the grand reception I get from the locals?"

Nitara reestablished the mask that hid her from the other vampires, allowing Graham to still see her. She didn't want to make a spectacle, something that was unavoidable if they could see her.

"Ah, they just don't know what brilliant company you make!" He sipped from his drink again. "Regarding my question, is there any chance that I'll get an answer this time?"

"Do I ever give you an answer?" She tilted her head and caught his smile from the corner of her eye. "What would make today any different?"

"I suppose, absolutely nothing." He shook his head and laughed at her expression. "Though it is unseasonably warm out."

"Unfortunately, the temperature has no bearing on my decision making!" She ran her finger along the rim of her glass and the empty vessel was full again. "But feel free to keep asking. I know you will."

"Of course I will! Just call me a hopeful fool." He tapped the bar to signal for another refill of his drink. "One of these days, you just might give in and tell me."

"You keep that hope alive." She lifted her freshly filled glass to his again before knocking back a second shot.

"You better take it easy." He sipped his drink slowly. "Can't be drunk on your first day back in action."

"Trust me, I am." After all she'd been through, she wanted a lot more than a couple of shots of whiskey, but it wasn't the time to drink away her woes ... at least Tyrellis didn't think so. So, of course, that meant she couldn't get sloppy with her alcoholic intake.

"Can I at least ask where you've been? I've missed seeing that somber face of yours around here." Graham dug in again as he tried to pull information from her. Nitara was used to his incessant questioning. It was what made him interesting. He was the only one she'd encountered who had enough balls to ask such bold questions of her.

"No place special." No, she had been nowhere worth bragging about. Just locked away in a dungeon, bound by the wishes of an asshole, and made to do terrible things that she could never forget.

"One of these days, you're going to let me in that little world of yours." He picked up the black cowboy hat that sat on the bar next to him and placed it on his bald head. Sensing the bullshit that was coming, Graham decided it was time for him to leave. He stood from the barstool and allowed his stocky height to tower over her.

Nitara turned her head, lifting her ear to the sound of an engine roaring outside of the door. "Yeah, one of these days." She smirked and abandoned her own seat.

"Catch ya later." The vampire grinned as he watched her cross the room until her figure faded to nothing. Nitara was planning a surprise entrance for the new arrivals. Laughing at the poor souls who would have to face her, he quickly exited the bar. Things were about to get sticky, and it would do him no favors to be around to witness it.

The rowdy group fell through the doors. Even though they were already completely intoxicated, the group still desired more. This was what she expected from most of the vampires who frequented the bars. They were self-indulgent and had no sense of personal limits. Nitara remained cloaked in the shadows as she watched them make complete fools of themselves. The bartender frowned as two of the drunken goofs fell on the bar and knocked a bowl of cherries onto the floor. Without so much as an apology, they pounded heavy fists on the bar and demanded service. The leader of their group—a tall, blond moron—laughed as he boasted about their latest roguish deeds.

"It's only a matter of time, boys!" he yelled as the previous patrons left. They wanted nothing to do with the chaos the group would undoubtedly cause. "Tyrellis is going down!"

"How many times have you said that shit, man? Cass, give it up! Tyrellis is the king and you're here drinking and dreaming with the rest of us," another smaller vampire with short, dark hair and eyes too big for his face joked.

Nitara chuckled from her shadowed position. Even she had heard the leader of the drunks give the same speech more times than she cared to count.

"Yeah, but the difference now is that his little genie bitch is gone! And I happen to know something that none of you do." He lowered his voice and narrowed his gaze. "He can't get her back!" Cass strutted across the bar to the empty table that sat in the center of the floor. Plopping his ass down into the worn chair, he leaned back and stretched out his arms and legs. "Our blessed petty king has run out of that convenient little fountain of luck!"

"What makes you so sure about that?" the odd faced vamp questioned as he hopped up onto a stool.

"I have my ways, and my sources. My guy on the inside tells me she is no longer his to command." He kicked his feet up onto the table. "We all know Tyrellis ain't shit without Nitara! Hell, he's a fucking baby compared to most of us. How else do you explain him being on top?"

The others nodded and grumbled; it was a common complaint. The oldest were always in power. That was how it had been since the very first vampires were made. Even before the order of the fae, vampires lived in a system of nests—each one reporting upward to a stronger nest, which was made of older vampires until the very top. Age determined the rule. When it came time, those who were of age could fight for the chance to lead. Barbaric perhaps, but it was their way.

"Is that why you stole her bike?" Mick, a frail vampire who held his arm around a human girl's shoulder, asked. In Reverie, the human population had become property. A tattoo tagged their owner's code on their neck. The rule was to check the tag before biting. Besides being fed on, they lived good lives because they said it made the blood taste better if the humans were fit and happy.

As a whole, the vampires took great care of the remaining human population. There were even a few farms which operated like resorts. In fact, some humans said that it was one of the best places for them to be in the new world order.

"I thought you grew some balls." Mick continued. "Guess the truth is just that you're no longer scared shitless of her because you know she isn't coming back!"

"I have never been afraid of that puppet!" Cass hissed at Mick, who simply laughed in response. "That's all she is. You know that. Right? She's a damn toy for him to play with! You can't be afraid of someone who has no control over their own actions!"

"Is that right?" Nitara appeared, cool strands of her signature purple smoke dancing around her and emphasizing her presence. "Don't I spark just the tiniest bit of fear in your heart, Cass?" She called him by his full name, the same as she'd done every time before, and he stiffened, just like always.

"Oh shit," the short vampire muttered, backing as far away from Cass as he could.

"Oh shit, is right." She winked at the short man before returning her attention to the one who'd so openly boasted about her inability to act as she pleased. "Cass, please, tell me one thing ..." She looked through the window to the sleek Harley that sat waiting. She hadn't seen it since Daegal had snatched her from her miserable existence for one that was far less appetizing. "Why do you have my bike?"

"Well, there was no point in letting it just sit there, wasting away until you returned." He laughed nervously. "Thought you would appreciate it being cared for."

"Oh, that I do. And now, you will return her to me." She held out her hand. "Keys."

Cass dug the keys out of his jeans pocket—still intact with the pink skeleton head—and handed them over to her. "See, no harm, no foul. I even had it cleaned today. We can just call this even, right?"

"Even? I don't know, Cass. I doubt I would call returning property taken from me without my consent, even. You stole from me, isn't that right?" Peering over his shoulder at the group watching them, she knew without a doubt that she would need to make an example of the vampire.

"Borrow, I borrowed from you!" He laughed nervously. "Borrowed, cleaned, and returned!"

"Semantics. Still, I can't just let you get away with that, free and clear. What message would that give to the others?" She circled him, boots tapping loudly against the floor. She snapped her finger, and the music stopped. The only sound was that of the nervous breaths of her target. "I mean, how does that sound? 'Feel free to steal from Nitara. She will just pat your back and let you off, as long as you return her belongings intact.' I don't know." Pausing in front of him, she rubbed her chin in thought. "No, I don't think that sounds good, do you?"

"I think it sounds fair." His lips spread around perfect white teeth. "Makes you sound easy going."

"Well, we're going to have to agree to disagree. Easy going isn't exactly the look that I'm going for." Nitara waved her finger and the chair beneath Cass dissolved into nothing; his legs straightened until he was upright, standing in front of her, against his own will. "So, let's discuss this puppet theory of yours. Tell me, how does it feel?"

"Look, I—" Cass began to plea, but his lips snapped tightly together. No matter how hard he tried to speak, he couldn't.

"Don't bother with begging. I'm not in the mood for it." She waved her hand and streams of purple smoke reached toward the terrified vampire as they turned into solid strands

14

that wrapped around him and restrained his movements. "You know what I *am* in the mood for? A puppet show!"

Nitara snapped her fingers, and Cass danced to the upbeat music that suddenly piped through the speakers. Laughing, she conjured another shot of whiskey, and then knocked it back. The others groaned as they watched their humiliated leader. Once satisfied with his performance, she snapped her fingers again and he fell to the floor. Nitara turned and strolled toward the exit, dragging the bound vampire behind her.

"What are you going to do to him?" Mick spoke up, giving voice to the fear they all shared.

"Oh, don't worry about our dear friend, Cass. We're going to go for a little ride. Considering how much our buddy here enjoys my bike, I thought he'd like one more chance to be with it! Would any of you care to join us?" She twirled her fingers and strands of purple smoke danced between them. Mick shook his head and moved out of her way as she exited the bar with her prisoner dragging behind her.

Once outside, Nitara admired the artwork that was her bike. Accented in purple, the beast stood under the moonlight in all its glory. She tied her haul on to the back of the bike and waved at the small crowd that formed around them. Straddling her baby for the first time in far too long, she grinned as it roared to life.

The sound of her hog had become her calling card in Reverie. The vamps knew it and got the hell out of dodge whenever it sounded off. As she pulled away from the bar, she grinned. What better way could she announce her return? What better way to reinstate the fear of the king's "puppet"? She drove through the center of Reverie where she knew everyone would see her.

Cass hung from the bike, floating behind her like a flag. This punishment was good, but not enough. She had to drive the point home. She continued following the road until the town and all the onlookers were behind them. Out in the center of the enormous field that separated Reverie from the surrounding towns, Nitara found a place to plant her flag. The light from the moon washed the scene in a calming glow that contradicted the panicked energy that bled from the vampire.

Nitara looked up at the sky; soon the sun would return, and he would be without cover. "Don't worry, you'll only burn a bit before the ropes dissolve. I trust you're full of blood and able to make it to hiding before it gets too bad." She winked. "Oh, and Cass, keep your damn hands off my bike!"

Cass choked on the dirt that was kicked up by the back tire of her bike as she drove away. Nitara didn't want to be in vamp land, but hell, if she had to be there, she was going to have some fun!

CHAPTER 2

Ardyn

"*I see you've retrieved your bike.*" Tyrellis sauntered into the calming atmosphere that was Nitara's room.

The vampire didn't always keep her trapped inside of the cold cavity of his chest. He said he didn't too much care for it, especially when she was in a 'mood'. It gave him headaches. Because of this slipped confession, Nitara made it her mission to get pile on the emotions whenever he forced her into his hollow core. It was the perfect time to drum up old traumas and work through them.

For the alternative, she created her own getaway. A room that brought her peace of mind. Images of the sun and moon danced on opposite walls. She draped seven large paned windows in sheer silk curtains that moved with the cool breeze coming through the open glass. Nitara sat in front of the open window at the small writing desk. She looked up from her scribblings and released her usual sigh of contentment for the unexpected guest.

"Yes, I have." As she spoke, the pen and paper she'd been using disappeared. "It was my right. I'm not even sure why Cass felt the need to pull such a stupid move to begin with."

Even if he thought she was away, why did he find it worth the risk? It was something that had been bothering her. It just didn't add up. The topic had become one of a priority for her. There was more to the story, and she needed to figure out what it was. She examined the bike thoroughly and nothing was out of place, not a single scratch.

"Isn't it obvious?" Tyrellis shrugged. "He was trying to prove a point. One that I think may have helped his cause against me." The vampire paused in thought as he toyed with the satin sheets covering her queen-sized bed. He nodded in approval of her decorative choice.

"You think so?" she asked.

"Never mind all that now. This turn of events will prove to benefit us! Now the heathens know that you're back. Perhaps they'll settle back into their place."

"Maybe." She smiled, but she knew nothing would stop Cass and his minions, not even the knowledge of her return. They wanted Tyrellis out, and that would not change.

Their leader's reckless behavior didn't help either. In all his time, Tyrellis had learned nothing about what it meant to lead. Whenever anything wasn't to his liking, he simply wished the problem away. What he couldn't change, however, was the discourse that was growing within the people who lived under his rule. And it was spreading like wildfire ... even more so since she'd been away. Without his endless supply of fulfilled wishes, Tyrellis had no way to mask his incompetence. The few who were on his side were turning their backs on him. And quickly.

"You don't think so?" He clapped his hands and the sound of the loud smack echoed off the ceiling. "I've heard of the display you made of dragging him through the town! Brilliant, simply brilliant. That will really make them think twice about crossing me again!"

She stood from her seat, crossed the large room, and got close up to the vampire, who stiffened. It wasn't often that Nitara neared him without his forcing the issue. "I think, with or without me on your side, there will be an uprising," she whispered close to his ear before she passed by him and moved to the bedside table.

"Yes, but with you by my side, they'll have no hopes of succeeding!" Tyrellis was just as sure of himself as she'd always known him to be. From the moment he took claim to the djinn, he was cocky and full of unearned confidence.

"If you believe so, then yes. Sure." She chuckled to herself. Men had a ridiculous ability of being so full of themselves, no

19

matter the species. It never ceased to amaze her. Tyrellis was no different.

"You think they could defeat you?" He chuckled—they both knew that no vampire, no matter the age, could stand against a djinn, especially Nitara. She was one of Daegal's prized achievements.

In his hopes of catching Jinn, he stumbled onto something much more satisfying. It was Nitara's love for her husband that made her all that more powerful. She was the key to his greatest plot. To take over the world. Unfortunately, the same love he looked to exploit was the thing that would become his greatest downfall.

"No, I don't think that." She paused, allowing him to have a moment of gloating before she squashed his hopes. "However, I'm not the only djinn left in existence, and Daegal's little stunt made sure the entire world knows it now. What's stopping them from going out and making a deal with another djinn to join them in their cause?"

"Why would any free djinn seek to aid vampires? There is no reason they would suddenly freely grant their wishes. And there is nothing a vampire can offer a djinn in trade that they can't conjure for themselves." Tyrellis had thought of every possibility.

The way he saw it, he was the only one to have claim to a djinn of his own. To him, it was an invaluable thing, one that guaranteed him an eternal life with his tight ass sitting perched on his golden throne on top of the world. You'd think a vampire of all people would know that all things come to an end. Even immortals.

"Well, you're holding me captive, not that anyone knows it ... yet. Once the word gets out, and it will, because the entire world now knows that I am alive, that may change things. Until now, my magic kept my presence hidden. Once vampires leave Reverie, they forget I exist. But now there are others out there who've seen me. Other djinn who will be looking for me." Nitara pulled at the threads of his logic, quickly unraveling his confidence. "Consider the fact that we djinn stick together. After all, there are so few of us. Perhaps they'd help just to get payback."

"We both know what happens to you if anything happens to me." He grinned, happy for the fail-safe the warlock had put in place when bonding the djinn to him. It meant that no one could touch him, including Nitara. Daegal realized she wouldn't love her new living arrangements, so he made it so if Tyrellis' life ended, so would hers.

"Yeah, you and I know the truth, but they don't." She stopped in front of him as she planted the seed of doubt in his mind. "Is that something you want to have publicized? Get rid of you and I'm no longer a threat. What's stopping them then from skipping right over the middleman?"

There it was, the piece that he hadn't considered. His enemies could very well avoid Nitara altogether and make a play to take Tyrellis out. It would eliminate two threats in one blow. That was the kicker. When Daegal bound Nitara to Tyrellis, he became her vessel. A soulless vampire was the perfect host. Living for an eternity and unable to be possessed by another.

"Leave me!" he yelled, frustrated with the turn of the conversation. "I need to think!"

"Whatever you say, boss." Ignoring the fact that they were in her room, she vanished from the space, leaving Tyrellis with his thoughts.

"Nitara, so good to see your face again!" The thick British accent of the dark-haired, green-eyed werewolf greeted her.

As he pulled back the long silk strands of hair that hung around his face, he turned to the entrance of his hidden home and welcomed the only other person who'd ever been inside. Nitara was one of the few who could pass through the barrier. They'd put a spell on the entrance, and it took the signature magic that djinn produced to unlock it.

This was something the collective of djinn came up with shortly after the wishes that granted their freedom. They needed a place to go without being bothered by the world. It wasn't often that they could move around without being bothered. Passersby in the streets felt it more than acceptable to bombard them with questions and wishes that, of course, would go unfulfilled. The escape became necessary when one such person thought it was okay to attack a djinn. This person didn't live for much longer afterwards, but the djinn decided that life in the open wasn't one that would ever work out. And so they went into hiding, creating magical spaces only they could access.

"Ardyn, good to see you're still hanging around here!" Nitara hugged the only person she could call a friend in the land of blood suckers.

Ardyn was a conundrum to the mind. His British accent contrasted with his oriental heritage. Born to an Asian father and an African American mother, he was predominantly raised by a British woman when his mother passed away as a young boy. Nitara reminded him of the pictures his father kept of his mother. It was why he trusted her.

She was worried that he would have gone elsewhere when Daegal forced her to leave Reverie. The man had no other friends, no ties, or reasons to stick around the vampire-infested lands. Ardyn was the only person she'd come in contact with that didn't drink blood to survive. When she was brooding over her new sentencing, chained to Tyrellis, she felt the magic of the hidden cavern where the unique man had built a home for himself. He was also in a shitty headspace thanks to Daegal's interference in his life. The dark warlock had a knack of ruining the lives of others.

"Where else would I go?" The tall, slender man returned the warm embrace. His lanky yet muscled arms wrapped around her, along with the musky smell of his other side. "Another ill-gotten experiment of our maker, Daegal. My dear, I'm here to stay!"

"Have you made any attempt to go home yet?" Nitara had hoped that if nothing else, in her absence, her hybrid friend would have found it in himself to escape the world of solitude. No matter what he said, she knew he resented the new life that was forced onto him. It went against his very nature.

"Home? No." He shrugged. "You and I both know that the wolves would never accept me. Not the way I am now." Moving away from her, he crossed the room filled with modern amenities to the massive double door refrigerator. From within, he grabbed two ice cold beers and tossed one to her. Cracking his open, he lifted it to her and took it to the head.

"How can you say that?" She sat next to him on the sofa facing a massive flat screened television. "You never even gave them a chance to prove you wrong."

"Nitara, look at me. I'm no longer a wolf, not really. It doesn't even feel the same when I shift anymore." Green eyes, the color of his wolf's fur, stared at her and broke her heart. It wasn't always that way, but after Daegal cast the spell that changed him, so was his wolf.

"I just think you should try. Living your life like this, just accepting it, is—"

"It's exactly what you're doing." He cut her off with a raised brow.

"Excuse me?" Rolling her eyes, she took a swig of her beer. This conversation was about to take a turn.

"Why didn't you tell Jinn you were here? Why wouldn't you let him help you?" It seemed her pal hadn't been completely out of the loop. Then again, he never was. The massive flat screen that hung on the wall wasn't there for the enjoyment of sports. It was his eyes and ears on the world around him. Nitara had apparently become one of his favorite channels.

"You know the answer to that as well as I do." She peered at him with suspicion, then her eyes flashed to the screen on the wall. "You were watching me the entire time?"

"Not the entire time. I tried, but I couldn't find you. Then a few days ago, you popped back up in the middle of a heavy battle. I was about to come to your aid when I saw you had plenty of help. Then I saw you with Jinn. And I turned the channel. Figured you'd stay there for a while, but here you are. And when I tuned back into his channel, he-"

She held her hand up to stop him. "I don't want to know. I can't be with him. That's all that matters. Leave it."

"Right, okay." He smiled ruefully. "But I think you should try to make it work with him. He clearly still loves you."

"And I think *you* should." She tossed the challenge back in his face. "I'm sure your people still love you as well."

"Looks like we've hit a stalemate." He shrugged before finishing his beer. He tapped the rim with his finger and the bottle was once again full.

"Looks like." She smiled. "So, what else is new around here? I see it's safe to assume you've been keeping up on everything."

"Not very much, same old. Cass and his gang are still plotting, but I think they are getting closer to an actual attempt at that hostile takeover. Things may get interesting soon." He grinned; it had been too long since he'd had something to pique his interest. The vampires were boring and predictable. A bit of switch up would be good for them.

"Good. I could use something to cut through the pain of being back here." She finished her beer, which was instantly refilled by a tap from her host. "Well, thank you."

"One would think you've had enough of interesting activity for a lifetime." He stretched his arms over his head and his shirt lifted, revealing his cut abs. "Besides, if they succeed, it likely means they'll kill Tyrellis. I want him out as much as the next person, but if he's out, it means ..." It was obvious he couldn't bring himself to finish the statement.

"It means I'm done with this mess, finally." She swallowed the beer in nearly one gulp before shaking it at him. He reached down and tapped it, refilling its contents.

"You can't mean that, Nitara." Ardyn pouted.

"I don't know what I mean anymore, not after everything that happened with Daegal and Jinn." Her chest tightened as she thought of Jinn. After all, he was still her husband, still the love of her life, and she would never see him again. Suddenly the beer in her hand didn't seem strong enough, so she waved her hand and a whiskey neat appeared. She knocked it back and sighed.

"You could still reach out." He pushed the topic yet again. "He's still out there, pining for you, no doubt. A call from you would make his day."

"I could, yes, but I won't." She was adamant, Jinn deserved to move on with his life without the burden of her mayhem. Either way, there was no chance of them ending up together. Besides, she couldn't be sure Tyrellis wouldn't know about it. If Tyrellis ever found out about Nitara attempting to contact her lost love, there was no telling what he would do to her or to him. The man was getting more reckless as time went on.

"Well, you know I'm down for whatever takes place. Just happy to have you back here." He growled playfully. "I was getting lonely!"

"In a strange way, I'm happy to be back. At least it means no more Daegal hanging over our heads." They'd all been living their lives in fear. When the warlock popped back on the playing field, every djinn went into hiding. It made no difference, though. He could hunt them all. The only ones who had eluded his efforts were Jinn, Rosie, Bruto, and Ardyn. Perhaps it was something to be said about them, something unique. Whatever it was, it had definitely bothered Daegal. During the time he held her captive, he'd chewed her ear off about it as if there was something she could do to change it.

"Cheers to that!" Ardyn boasted. They lifted their drinks in the air—this was going to be a night full of booze. "You know, I'll never get used to this." He tapped his drink once more, and the bottle was again full. "I've been this way for nearly three decades now, and yet, I still find it odd."

"Oh, yeah, you'll get used to it, trust me." She laughed as she watched him eye the bottle and wondered how many times he'd done that parlor trick before she got there. There was another bottle on the table next to her that didn't belong to her. Ardyn was in a good mood, one aided by a liquid booster. "Just be glad he never got around to assigning you a vessel. That is the absolute worst. Losing control at the whim of a bottle, it's so depreciating. Here I am again, tied to a bottle. Only this one can actually order me around!"

"You know, I think my wolf was supposed to be that. Daegal must have thought he could control the man by controlling the animal. However, it seems he made a miscalculation. I'm a mature wolf and therefore, I learned a long time ago to control the beast and not let it control me, so I guess that bit backfired on him."

"Part werewolf, part djinn." She shook her head in disbelief. In her life, she'd seen a lot of things, but Ardyn was something that fascinated her. "You truly are one of a kind. I wonder how many others out there are like you. Creations of oddity."

"Oddity, huh?" He laughed at her phrasing. "Well, a lot of good it's doing me right now. I live in what is basically a dungeon, completely away from the world. Hell, I haven't gotten laid in longer than I care to admit to you."

"I won't beat the topic to death, but living here like this is your choice. There is nothing keeping you here, especially now that Daegal is gone." She winked at him. "All the lady wolves are out there howling at the moon. They're just waiting for the magic that is Ardyn."

"You know, you can really pour it on thick when you want to." He frowned at her.

"How about you pour some more of that magical elixir? I think this is a night to drink away. Besides, we should celebrate the return of sunshine to your dreary little world."

"And sunshine would be?"

"Well, me of course!" she said with a straight face that held for only a moment. Then the two broke out in laughter and the drinks poured freely.

After his fifteenth drink, though the count was fuzzy, Ardyn watched a woman also lost in her own thoughts. "Look, what if I told you there may be a workaround to your problem? A way to get you out of this thing with Tyrellis, without hurting you. There may be something you hadn't thought of."

"A work around?" His words pulled her from her thoughts. "What do you mean?"

"Yes, I mean that with a little help, you could be free of this without sacrificing yourself." He straightened. "Nitara, I know you're all ready to throw yourself on the sword here, but I would hate for that to happen. Trust me when I say Jinn wouldn't be the only one to miss you."

"I take it you've been working something out?" She asked, a tinge of hope in her voice.

"Yes, as a matter of fact, I have. And I kinda need to not tell you any more than this. Just in case Tyrellis wishes information from you. I just need you to agree to let me try. I considered doing this without your approval, but that somehow didn't seem right."

"So, this is to be a rescue mission that I'm left in the dark about?" She asked. "I don't know if I like that."

"Yes, for now. I know you like to be in control, but if this is going to work, you can't be." He explained. "That much is necessary. I'm sure you understand."

"And what do you expect me to do in the meantime?"

"Keep being the badass peace keeper he wants you to be." He laughed. "Perhaps drag a few more vampires through the streets? That was hilarious to watch!"

"That's something I can do." She smiled widely as she thought of the man she left strung out in the field. She had only just considered if he escaped with any skin left on his ass.

"So, do you agree?" Ardyn waited with an eager and pleading look on his face.

She paused, thinking of her love, Jinn. If there was a chance she could be with him again, why shouldn't she take it? She trusted Ardyn, and if he thought he found a way, well, she had faith in his instinct. "Yeah, I agree ... If you agree to go home again once all of this is done."

"Dammit, had to have a catch, huh?" Ardyn shook his head. "Can't just let me help you?"

"You help me, and I help you. That's what friends are for."
She smiled. "So?"

"So, I guess we have ourselves a deal. It's not like I'm going to let you stay like this just to avoid facing my family. I promise to try. That's it."

"That's good enough for me."

The two shook on the agreement before the liquor started to flow again. They had a lot to celebrate, and a lot to worry about. Whiskey seemed a solid solution for both.

CHAPTER 3

Alliances

"Inda, it's good to see** you again." Graham flexed his muscles as he stood on the edges of Tyrellis' land. He hadn't expected to see the woman he'd been friends with since her return to Earth. "Still haven't returned to your dragon, I see."

He turned to the woman, who landed softly on the ground behind him, carried by wings of fire. Inda was a phoenix. When the wars of Earth started, all of her kind were called to return home. It'd been about a decade since they lifted the ban, allowing the fiery birds to cross realms and return to their world.

"No, not quite." She shifted, and the wings of fire folded into her back, allowing her arms to relax at her sides.

"Why is that?" He smiled as he started in with his usual teasing. "I expected the two of you to be honeymooning by now."

"Is there a reason you're so intent on my returning to him? I thought you and I enjoyed each other's company, the loners that we are." Crossing her arms over her chest, she tapped her foot on the ground. "If you'd prefer I leave, I will."

"You know I enjoy every minute of your company." He laughed at her angry face. "Now, settle down. You and I both know I couldn't help myself. The return of your beloved to your life, and yet you're still flying around here."

"And yet, you're intent on sending me to the land of dragons." She thought of the man he spoke of.

Jax was the prince of the dragons and desperately seeking to reconnect with her. If it hadn't been for Briar, her big-mouthed friend and now the Queen of the fairies, he'd still be unaware of her return. Now that he knew she was back in the realm that formerly belonged to the humans, he was searching for her. Hence her return to the one place he wouldn't go, Reverie. Jax absolutely hated vampires.

"I just want everyone to be happy, and as much as you put on your brave face, I know you aren't content lurking around here." Graham could tell that Inda wanted to be with her jilted lover, but foolish pride stood in her way. Time would take that away from her, he hoped. Though the woman was older than he could guess—and older than she would ever admit—all the years under her belt and she was still just as bullheaded.

"Perhaps." She damn near looked at the back of her own skull as she expressed her annoyance with the man with an exaggerated eye roll. Graham was worse than her own father with the lectures in life lessons. He meant well. She knew it, but she wanted nothing to do with it.

"And yet you stay because you know that this is the one place he won't come looking for you." Not only did Jax detest the vampires, the vampires had also made enemies of just about every species on the planet. For that reason, they were left alone. Everyone knew that if nothing else, the treaty with the fae would keep them in check. It made no sense to antagonize the situation any further.

"Can we change the subject, please?" She feigned a yawn, covering her mouth with her hand and again rolling her eyes again. It was something she did often, because it annoyed him just as much as his fathering bothered her.

"Of course we can!" He smiled. "Anything for you!"

"What brings you out here?" Inda had been flying overhead when she spotted him. "Not that I'm not happy about the pleasant surprise. It's been quite a while since we've hung out. This just isn't one of your usual spots, so out in the open."

"You're right. Usually I would be in hiding, away from the public space, but I'm here waiting on a friend." Graham had gotten a call from a familiar voice, one that claimed to have a deal he wouldn't be able to refuse. Otherwise, standing outside on a hill overlooking the city sounded like a terrible time. Just in the distance, he could see right into the bedroom of the man the entire country wanted to take out. At least it seemed he was enjoying the night.

"Impossible. You did not know I would be here." She grinned. Graham wasn't what you would call a popular guy. No one bothered him, but there wasn't exactly a line of people bidding for the top spot on his buddy list.

"Look at the ego on you." He laughed. "You know, I have enough charm to grunge up more than one person who appreciates spending time in my company."

"Oh, I'm sure of it." She looked over her shoulder. "What time were you planning to meet this mysterious friend?"

"Soon. Come to think of it, he should be here already." Graham grunted. "I wonder what's taking so long."

"Perhaps your date stood you up." She winked and her laughter rang out into the night.

"Am I interrupting something here?" Ardyn spoke from behind them, appearing in a puff of green and black smoke. "I'd hate to disrupt whatever would cause such a delightful sound."

"Well, aren't you the charmer?" Inda greeted the newcomer before turning to Graham. "You know, you could stand to learn a thing or two from him about how to treat a lady."

"Ah, there he is, the mysterious Mr. Ardyn." Graham was one of the few people who knew about Ardyn and what he was.

It was purely by accident that Graham spotted the shifter when he touched down in Reverie. Ardyn was running from

Daegal. The warlock had been trying to trap the wolf after his failed creation got away from him. It was Graham who showed him to the path to the hidden cavern he made all his own. The vampire knew a lot about the djinn's magic, and until Nitara came into his life, Ardyn relied on Graham to help him figure it all out.

"In the flesh." Ardyn smiled and flared his arms—a grand gesture not lost on his friend.

"Ardyn, this is Inda. Inda, Ardyn." Graham made the proper introductions.

"It's nice to meet you." Ardyn flashed his handsome smile at Inda, whose face warmed.

Even with his time away from the general population, Ardyn still had a certain effect on women. Inda was a shifter, which made her more susceptible to his particular charms. Becoming djinn turned that allure into something more intense. Imagine his surprise when a panther in heat chased him down. That had to be the most thrilling part about his escape from Daegal.

"You know, you take up interesting companions, Graham. Djinns, wolves, and a lovely phoenix." Ardyn flirted easily. "You must tell me how you do it, being that you're one of the most hated species around."

"I'll tell you my secret when you tell me why you've called me out here to meet," Graham smirked. He could smell the arousal, the sexual tension between the two of them, and he wanted to bring that to an end, or get the hell away from them should it turn into something more tantalizing.

"Yes, our dilemma." Ardyn paced, pensively looking at the unexpected addition to their gathering. He sized her up as he wondered if she could be trusted.

"And that is?" Graham noticed Ardyn's hesitation. Of course, the man was ready to take her to bed, but couldn't tell her a secret. "Look, Inda is good. You can trust her. If not, she wouldn't be here."

"If you trust her, I suppose it is okay." Ardyn agreed. "I'm here about Nitara."

"Nitara? What about her?" Finally, Ardyn had said something worthy of grasping Graham's attention.

"She wants out, and I intend to help make that happen." Ardyn's chest lifted with pride.

"She wants out of what exactly?" Graham did not know the hold Tyrellis really had over Nitara. It was the bit of information he'd been trying, unsuccessfully, to get out of her for years.

"Her arrangements with Tyrellis." Ardyn had contemplated just how much he should reveal to the man he'd hoped would become an ally in his efforts to save his friend.

"Wait, Nitara, as in the djinn formerly married to Jinn?" Inda's mind was piecing the information together quickly. "She's here in Reverie?"

"You know about her?" Ardyn asked. It wasn't that shocking that she knew who they were talking about, considering they were in vampire territory where Nitara was a known enforcer.

"Yes, as a matter of fact, I do." Inda's shoulders squared with a sudden tension as her suspicion was confirmed. She met Graham's eyes. "She just happens to be the reason Jax knows that I've returned here. If it weren't for Jinn trying to save her, I'd still be free and clear."

"Oh, you're *that* Inda." Ardyn smiled, recognizing the name of her ex-lover.

"You know who I am?" Inda tensed; the recognition wasn't something she cared for.

"Yes, well, it would appear we live in a very small world. Even with all this separation, it seems we're all still just as entangled in each other's lives." Ardyn's eyes danced as he thought of other ways they could become entangled, dragon prince ex-boyfriend looming in the shadows or not.

"Why doesn't she just leave if she wants out?" Graham was tired of the intermission from Ardyn getting to the point of their meeting. If the two of them wanted to play seven degrees of supernatural, they could do it another time. "Why is all of this subterfuge necessary?"

"Let's just say it's not as easy as her just deciding to leave. There is a contract between them that's not easily broken. If you could imagine, this isn't exactly a life she would so readily sign up for. In any matter, even though she wants to leave, it isn't as simple as just getting up and walking away from Tyrellis. But I believe that I have found a way around that. I'll need your help, and Inda, if you're interested, you could play an interesting part in all of this as well." His mind worked quickly, recalculating the way things would play out. He hadn't planned to include another party in their ploy, but now that she was there and privy to his thoughts, he figured she might prove a useful resource.

"Why in the hell would I want to help you?" Still sour about the events that led to her permanent exile to Reverie, Inda saw a grudge and was eager to grab hold of it.

"Same question goes for me." Graham turned the focus back to him. "What makes you think I'd be so eager to help?"

"Inda, I honestly can't say that you have any reason to help us. I hope you'll do it from the kindness of your heart, which I can tell is a caring one, despite the sour look you're giving me at the moment." Ardyn cleared his throat. "And Graham, I'd think that for you, it would be obvious. If this works out, it means Tyrellis will be without his djinn, and unable to keep you from taking your rightful place as the head of this nest. That is why you hang around, isn't it? You're the oldest, strongest vampire out there. That much I can tell by how you waltz in and out of there without so much as a scratch. Those vampires respect you. When Tyrellis is down, there will be a move for the throne. Who better to take his place than you? Unless you're ready to live under the rule of that idiot, Cass."

"What is it you would need from me?" Graham had heard enough to consider what the man was offering. It hadn't been lost on him, the chance to take over. Ardyn had hit the nail on the head, even if it was unintentional. Tyrellis was a child compared to the older vampire, Cass, not much better than that. If it hadn't been for the djinn in the pocket of the current leader, it would be Graham at the head.

Markus, the former leader of the vampires, had just announced his plans to go to ground. It was what vampires did when they grew tired of the world. Some would set a timeframe, an ending to their slumber. Markus, however, had made it perfectly clear that he no longer wished to be awakened. He preferred the slumber to the realities of what the world had become. Because Markus was stepping down, there was no fight for the opportunity to replace him. He was to name a predecessor.

All of Reverie murmured with the rumors that Graham was that person. He was the strongest, bravest, and hell, Markus loved him. Tyrellis, however, was a nobody. Before that night, most of the vampires had never even heard of him. Yet, he waltzed into the room with a djinn by his side and Markus announced him as the new leader of Reverie. There was nothing that could be done, not then, and not since. Not as long as he had her. Overnight, Reverie turned into his playground and those who opposed simply headed for the outskirts.

Yes, there were attempts made on his life, but none that succeeded. Once they realized Nitara would do whatever the vampire commanded, they had all but given up hope. Graham took a different approach to the issue—instead of running, he stayed. He kept a low profile, but in time got to know Nitara, who showed that she wanted no more to do with Tyrellis than the people she forced to follow him.

"I take it that means you will help?" Ardyn waited for the confirming nod from Graham before he clapped his hand and turned to Inda. He hoped she would follow the lead of the old vampire.

"If Graham is in, I guess I am, too." Inda nodded before he could ask. "Besides, it's so damn boring around here."

"Great. I need you to get a message to Jinn, and with no one knowing about it. This was a task I was going to take on, but if you join our little endeavor, it means I can stay here and move ahead with the rest of the plan." It would also mean fewer questions for Ardyn to answer about who and what he was. Jinn and everyone else in fairy land already knew Inda. She was best friends with the queen, so odds were she'd be able to fly in and out with no problems. Ardyn, on the other hand, would set off all sorts of magical alarms the moment he left Reverie.

"What's the rest of the plan?" Graham questioned while Inda thought over the request.

"Now, you know I can't tell you everything up front." Ardyn laughed. "All in due time, my friend. What I need now is confirmation that you will help, now that you know you'll benefit from this as well. That nod of yours is nice, but I need to hear the words so I can hold you to it."

"Then we're back to the question of why I should help you." Graham played it cool. "Hell, I can just wait until you succeed, or fail, and make my move then."

"Yes, you could do that, but I know your secret." Ardyn leaned in and raised a brow at the vampire. "That thing you don't want anyone to know."

"Yeah, what's that?" Graham bristled at what sounded like a threat.

Ardyn held his hands up. "Hold on, buddy, it's nothing like that." When Graham relaxed, he continued. "You love her. Nitara. And you want to make sure that she is okay, just as I do."

"Love her?" Graham laughed. "You're off your rocker."

"I doubt that. I've been watching you. The entire time she was away, you didn't set one foot in that bar. And yet, the moment she returned, there you were again with your witty banter and elusive ways." He paused, weighing his next words. If he was wrong, it would mean spilling Nitara's secret. He trusted Graham, though, and if he wasn't convincing enough, the man would never help them. "Not only that, but I suspect you know a bit more about her secret than you care to let on. You know what I plan to avoid in doing all this."

"I don't know what the hell you're talking about." Graham refused his claim.

"I'd believe that, but you've never acted against him. The entire time she was away, you could have made your move on Tyrellis, ended his life, but you knew it would mean ending hers as well." There it was, the truth, written all over Graham's face. He had known it even if it she never gave him the confirmation he needed. "In fact, a little birdy told me you saved Tyrellis, the night Nitara's bike was stolen. Cass was there to take his life, and instead he walked away with a bike as his consolation prize. I suspect you threw your age around. Perhaps you made the younger vampire think you were making your move when, in fact, you were not."

"You seem to know a lot about things you should know nothing about." Graham tightened his jaw. "How is that?"

"I'm a djinn. You know its easy for me to gather information. I know a lot more than most." Ardyn took another step back. "I also know that Nitara means a lot to both of us. We can't let her continue to suffer like this."

"So, what if I do care for her? There are many people I've cared for in my lifetime. It never meant I would lay my life on the line for them."

"See, I doubt you care for that many people. How could you when you barely let anyone get close to you? Which tells me the fact that you allow that closeness to exist with her most definitely means you're going to help me save her. Even though if we succeed, you'll likely never see her again. She will leave here and never return to you." That much wasn't in question. If they could save Nitara, she would go back to Jinn, back to where she really wanted to be.

"Okay, so he saves the girl he apparently cares so much for. You save a friend. What's in it for me?" Inda spoke up. She'd been debating her position. For her, there was no valuable stake in the game. If Ardyn was expecting her to operate strictly from the kindness of her heart, he had a rude awakening coming. If not for an untimely spotting of Graham, she wouldn't have even been in on the conversation. "I'm starting to reconsider my easy agreement to your request. Those green eyes must have put a spell on me."

"Not sure, but what else do you have going on right now?" Ardyn flashed a smile—as far as he could tell, she wasn't exactly a social butterfly. He hadn't caught her on his radar which meant she'd been inactive. "Besides, Jinn and Jax have become pretty close. Perhaps while you're there, you could speak to your ex."

"That's not exactly going to convince her to make the journey." Graham laughed as Inda's face turned red. It was all the bird could do not to go up in flames.

"What do you mean?" Ardyn asked.

"He means I'm in no rush to see my ex again." Laughing, she shook her head. "It's hard to believe you hadn't caught on to that."

"Well, that seems like an odd lie to tell." Ardyn frowned.

"Excuse me?" The bird was heating up and if he didn't calm her down, she could cause major problems for them.

"Look, I meant no harm, but I can hear the change in your heartbeat at the mention of his name, and I can see in your eyes that you aren't as over him as you would have the world believe. I'm sure Graham here can tell the same, yet perhaps he is wiser than I, and didn't put his foot in his mouth by saying it to your face."

"Well, it may be a good idea for you to follow suit," she huffed.

"Look, you're here, and we could really use your help, so what do you say?" Ardyn was done trying to convince her to help. Either she would or she wouldn't. His plan didn't depend on her participation.

Inda looked at Graham, who seemed to agree. If not for the pathetic expression on the vampire's mug, she would have told both of them to kiss her ass. "Fine, whatever. What's the message?" It'd been a while since she'd been to the area. Perhaps she could pay her friend, Briar, a visit and thank her for inviting new drama into her life.

CHAPTER 4

Kiss Off

"Graham, we meet again, and so soon."** Nitara took her usual spot on the bar stool next to the somber-looking vampire. "You look a little more down than usual. Is there something bothering you?"

"Yes, it looks like we can't get enough of each other." He removed the hat from his head. "And, yes, there is always something running through this old mind of mine. You'd think after so long on this planet, I would have gone through every thought possible. But it's just as noisy in here as ever."

"Maybe. Or maybe you use that as an excuse to come in here and get more of what's flowing from those taps." She laughed as she pointed to the glass in his hand. "How many of those have you had tonight?"

"What can I say? They have the good stuff." The truth was, there were plenty of places that had higher quality product to offer, but they didn't have as much drama, which meant Nitara wasn't a regular there. He had to go where he knew he had a chance of seeing her.

"I suppose. So, how have things been around here? Quiet?" Nitara hadn't been back to the bar since her interaction with the ringleader of the local outlaws. Instead, her rounds took her to local businesses and functions where Tyrellis should have been in attendance. He'd sent her in his place, to make a statement ... the wrong statement, but who was she to question his decision making?

"Well, after your last display, I'm surprised there are still customers at all." He laughed as she noted the grunt from the bartender, who clearly agreed with his assessment. Of course, profits would suffer momentarily, but the drunkards always returned.

"I had a point to prove." Nitara shrugged and adjusted the collar of her leather jacket.

"That you did." Lifting his drink from the dark bar top, he called attention to her not having a drink of her own. "Care to join me for a drink? I promise not to pry this time."

"What the hell. I could use a break." Nitara had spent her day watching over the new vampire pups. Every year the vampires chose a select few to turn—not enough to harm the human to vampire ratio, but enough to keep things interesting, as the idiot who pulled her strings often found it necessary to make examples out of the younger vampires. It also helped with population control. The vampires were immortal, but often their fights turned deadly.

"A hard-working woman like yourself deserves one more than anyone else in this place." He looked around the bar and saw the dark room had very few patrons inside. "Not that there are a lot of people here."

"When you're right, you're right." She drank from the glass that appeared in her hand. The dark liquid warmed her as it invaded her body. Winter was quickly approaching, and she was no fan. How she wished she could be on a beach somewhere with an umbrella drink in her hand. "Of course the vampires would take over former Canada. It's too damn cold here."

"You're a djinn. Warm yourself up." Graham joked. "Tell me something. Are you planning on hanging around for good now?"

"Did you miss me that much while I was away?" She batted her eyes and teased him. "Are you afraid I'll leave you again?"

"Well, considering you're the only one who talks to me when I'm here, yes, I did." He pointed at the bartender, who pretended not to be listening. "Even this guy, barely a word spoken, no matter how many drinks I order."

"Well, it looks like you're in luck. I doubt I'll be going anywhere for quite some time. So you'll have someone to talk to for as long as you want." Of course, that wasn't her choice by any means.

"It doesn't seem like you're all that happy about it." He stated the obvious.

"Would you be?" She rolled her eyes.

"Nitara—"

"Graham, you said no prying. Remember?" She nudged him in the arm. "It was just a few minutes ago. I can't believe you've forgotten already!"

"Look, if something was wrong, you'd tell me, right?" He lowered his voice to barely a whisper. "If you were in trouble and needed help, I hope you know you could count on me."

"What makes you think something is wrong?" Nitara frowned and leaned away from him. He'd never crossed the line into a genuine concern for her wellbeing. "Where is this coming from, Graham?"

"I know we aren't that close, not that you're all that close with anyone around these parts, but I'd like to think we're friends. Despite your obvious aversion to my kind." Again, he quieted himself. "Just know that if you need anything, I'm here."

"Thanks, Graham. I'm glad to know that you'd be there, but I'm a big girl. I can handle myself." The conversation felt far too familiar. Graham had always been nosey, but this was on another level entirely. "What brought on this topic?"

"What do you mean?" He tapped the bar, requesting a refill. "I'm just as curious about you as I've always been. There's no difference today."

"No, this is different. Usually you're concerned with the reason behind why I'm here, as if trying to solve some mystery. This is different, though." She scrutinized his face. His jaw tightened, his eyes flickered between her and the bartender. Graham was worried. "Suddenly, you're trying to help me. I'm left wondering what brought on the idea that I would need your help."

The eyes of the bartender, glued to his forehead, stopped Graham from speaking. Nitara certainly wasn't the only person who acted as a messenger for Tyrellis. Realizing that they weren't in what he would consider a safe space, he opted to cut their conversation short. "I don't know what you mean. Look, I have to go." He abruptly stood and headed for the exit, but as he walked by her, he pulled her hand into his, and slipped her a note. Nitara made the note disappear before the observant bartender could see it.

Nitara stayed behind, nursing her drink after he left her. She couldn't be too quick to leave. Not with the overly intrigued bartender watching her. Every now and then, she would see his eyes dart to her as he no doubt speculated about the relationship between her and the vampire who'd already left the bar. A few others also watched her; she could hear their whispers, all of course assuming the wrong thing, the predictable thing, that she and Graham were more than just friends.

Nitara was sure that was his intention with the way he delivered his hidden message to her. The way his fingers lingered at her wrist and caressed the skin there for a moment; there was so much an audience could take from such an insignificant gesture. They would all see it and assume it was a sign of his affection for her. The man was smart. She had to give him that much.

Once free of watchful eyes, the note reappeared, still intact. She sat on her hill looking out at the city as she pulled it from her pocket. What could he have to say to her that was so important he thought it worth the risk of rousing the suspicion of those he knew would run back to Tyrellis? Was that what he wanted to happen? Did he want to use her to get to the king? If nothing else, it would cause a definite bout of paranoia for the young vampire who already feared his life and position were at stake.

As she assumed, the note held a simple request, one that he'd been able to get to her before in far less conspicuous ways. Graham was playing a game, and Nitara didn't appreciate being an unwilling pawn. Still, she followed through and give him what he asked for. Emptying her lungs and watching the exasperated air dance in the night's chill, she drew him to her mind and let his essence pull her to his location.

"What is this about?" Nitara appeared inside of a building that had clearly been abandoned for quite some time. The air was stale, and dust and cobwebs covered every surface and corner.

"There are too many ears at the bar, and I needed to speak with you freely." Graham stood in the center of an empty room. His expression was more serious than she'd ever seen before.

"You're playing a really dangerous game here." Nitara refused to sit on anything in the decaying structure. Most of the broken-down furniture looked like it couldn't hold the weight of a flea. Instead, she waved her hand, and in the middle of the room appeared one plush chair. She walked over to it and sat down.

"Really?" Graham laughed at her. "I think Tyrellis is rubbing off on you."

"Oh, shut up! I'm tired." She waved her hand again and a small pink stool covered in yellow flowers appeared in front of him. "There, happy now?"

"Very funny." Graham kicked the stool meant for a child away from him.

"Yes, I thought so." She laughed, but they had more important things to discuss. "You know, if I didn't know better, I'd think you wanted to make a point with that little show."

"I don't know what you mean." He played stupid.

"Sure you don't." With another flick of her hand, an adult sized chair appeared directly across from her. This time, Graham accepted the offered seat. The two watched each other for a moment after he sat. "So, are you going to tell me what you want?"

"I know things are not as they seem." Graham admitted cryptically. "I just wanted to help."

"Help?" She straightened. "Why do you suddenly think I need help? Where is this coming from?"

"Never mind." He trained his eyes on her figure. "I need to know something."

"What's that?" Nitara frowned. She couldn't tell what was going on with him, but suddenly she felt uncomfortable with his eyes on her.

Graham got up from his seat, crossed the small space, and lingered in front of her. When she didn't move, he lowered himself and his hands braced his weight on the armrests at her side. Nitara didn't flinch. He searched her eyes, but she couldn't tell what he was looking for. When she thought to speak, to question his intention, it was too late. His lips pressed against hers with an urgent sadness that had no explanation.

Nitara allowed the kiss to linger for a moment before she pulled away. She looked at him with a blank expression. "What was that about?"

"Sorry, I've been wanting to do that for a while now." He dropped his head and stepped away. Her expression confirmed what he already knew, but didn't want to accept. She had no feelings for the man in front of her.

"Look, I'm not interested in hooking up in this dungeon, if that's what you had in mind. Being alone all these years is tough, I'll admit it, but I'm not that touch deprived yet." Standing, Nitara moved away from Graham just enough to prove her point. "I only came because I thought you wanted to talk."

"I do." He shook his head. "That's why I asked you to come. To talk, I just got lost in the moment."

"So talk and keep your lips on your side of the room, please." She smiled, but the expression didn't soften the blow of her rejection. Graham's face twisted with her words.

"Damn, was it that bad? Look, okay, I get it." He held up his hands. "Keeping my hands and my lips to myself."

"I'm sorry, but we're friends. That's it. I—" Nitara felt the stab of guilt. She hadn't meant to be so cold towards the man. His actions had caught her off guard.

"Yeah, I know, you've only got eyes for Jinn," Graham admitted bluntly.

"How do you know about him?" She bristled. Graham knew a lot more than he was letting on. It made her wonder just how much he wasn't telling her.

"You're kidding, right? Everyone knows, but no one talks about it, at least not in front of you. There are literally bets going on about how long it will take for you to drop this shit with Tyrellis and go back to him." Graham was perhaps one of the few people who wasn't rooting for a happy reunion. Of course, he was the only vampire who wanted the djinn to stick around despite her aiding Tyrellis in his takeover.

"I honestly hadn't considered it. No one ever mentioned it, so I assumed Daegal erased the memory of us from the world. It wouldn't be unlike him. He hated what we had." She paused and frowned at the idea that everyone around her knew just how miserable she really was. They all knew that she wanted to be away from there, with the love she'd been longing for. Did they pity her? Did they joke about her pain? Apparently, it was a thing of amusement, considering there were bets being placed. "Graham, I'm sorry. I just can't go down this road with you, or anyone else, for that matter. Not even Jinn."

"No, don't worry about it." Graham had to save face and turn the conversation around. He hated the look in her eyes—it was pity. Great, the first woman he'd tried to approach in years and she only felt sorry for him. "Look, I know you want to get the hell out of Reverie. For whatever reason, one you refuse to share with me, you can't leave. I just want you to know that I'm on your side, Nitara."

"This conversation feels way too familiar." There it was, the understanding. She knew exactly where his sudden interest in saving her was coming from. "Fucking Ardyn! He got to you, didn't he?"

"I-," Graham hesitated just a moment too long and Nitara snapped.

She snapped her fingers and yelled the name of the man who apparently struggled to keep a secret. "Ardyn!"

"You called?" Ardyn appeared in the corner in a flare. Once he got a look at their drab surroundings, he frowned. "Where the hell are we?"

"You told him?" Nitara questioned in a huff. "How could you? You know, you have such a big mouth!"

"Look, I didn't tell him anything. I simply asked for his assistance in helping me rid you of an inconvenient problem. That's all." He crossed the room to stand by a shamed Graham's side. "Anything outside of that, if he knows anything at all, he got that without my help. I know better than to go blabbing your secrets to the world!"

"You expect me to believe that he agreed to help you without knowing why?" She looked at Graham. "Why would you do that?" Even if he had an infatuation with her, there had to be more to the story.

"Because, if we succeed, and we will, our pal Graham here will become the new vampire ruler," Ardyn answered her question and slapped the vampire on the shoulder, but quickly pulled his hand away when Graham sneered. They were cool, but apparently not cool enough for physical contact. "He's the oldest and baddest vampire around here. It only makes sense."

"You've got to be kidding me!" Nitara paced the floor. "How could you involve me in this? Do you know what risk you put not only me, but the two of you in? What do you think Tyrellis will do when he finds out about this? Hell, if Graham is as strong as you say, he's already on the radar. And you're supposed to be in hiding. Why would you take this risk?"

"Look, I told you, I'm taking care of it." Ardyn narrowed his eyes at Graham. "You weren't supposed to tell her anything."

"I didn't tell her anything. You did," Graham corrected him. "I'm smarter than you want to give me credit for."

"You didn't think this little conversation was going to be enough for her to put two and two together?" Ardyn snapped his fingers in Graham's face. "You're so smart, but you didn't see that?"

"Look, I—" Graham frowned as Ardyn cut him off.

"You just wanted to take your shot, I get it, but you've kinda screwed us. Nitara was to be left in the dark, so she could honestly deny anything if questioned about it."

"Shit." Graham looked at Nitara, who rolled her eyes. "I'm sorry. I didn't think about that."

"Yeah, that much is obvious." Ardyn punched him in the arm and then popped to the opposite side of the room to escape any retaliating blow.

"Look, I'm just going to leave now. Technically, all I know is that the two of you are fucking idiots, and that's not new information." Nitara rolled her eyes and vanished from the room.

"Seriously, what were you thinking?" Ardyn dropped his joking manner. With Nitara out of the room, they could have a serious discussion about what happened. "Did you think you could convince her to stay here with you?"

"I don't know what I thought." Graham kicked the chair that Nitara had conjured and sent it flying across the room. "I don't want her to go. Hell, she's been one of the few people I could talk to and rely on through this entire mess. Even if she didn't know it, I counted on seeing her. That time when she was away, doing god knows what, I missed her like crazy. And now, I'm just supposed to let her walk out of my life without even trying to prevent it?"

"You know you two can't be together." Ardyn couldn't believe what he was hearing. He'd known that Graham cared about Nitara, but he didn't know his feelings were that deep.

"Yeah, I know." Staring at the empty seat where he'd kissed her lips, Graham sighed. It was the first and last time he would do that, but dammit if it wasn't good for him. If only she'd enjoyed it as much as he did. "Fuck."

"Sorry, man. But hey, once you're the boss, you'll have all the bloodsucking babes throwing themselves at you." Ardyn snapped his fingers and in front of them, hanging in the air, appeared the display of a fictional future. They watched the image of a smiling Graham, sitting on Tyrellis' throne with a busty vampire in his lap. "So much that you won't even be able to remember who Nitara is."

"Oh, I could get used to that." They both knew Ardyn was a liar, but dammit if the image he created wasn't a good one.

CHAPTER 5

Acts of Desperation

As she walked around the complex, Nitara kept a close eye on the vampires in Tyrellis' keep. It didn't take a genius to see that most of them weren't to be trusted. They were only there because of the protection Nitara gave them. While she was away, more than half of the bastards had defected. They left the compound in order to get away from attacks they were sure were going to happen. In the short time that she had been back, they were there again. Snuggling up under the safety net. Tyrellis was a joke, and if nothing else made that clear, the company he kept did. Like a moron, he let them all right back in with little to no consequences for their lack of loyalty to him. That alone weakened his position more than he knew.

The vampires who hung around were the weakest she'd seen. Cass and his guys would have had no problem taking them down on an even playing field. As long as she was in the picture, that would never be the case. She hadn't seen or heard from her immortal vessel since their last conversation. Perhaps he was in hiding, fearing that she would tell someone his dirty secret. Even though he held the power to control what she did, including the information she relayed to others, he still worried that she would betray him. If there was a magical loophole to her situation, she hadn't found it yet.

As it was, Ardyn figured it out on his own and because of those damn magical cameras. He'd seen Tyrellis pull her into his chest and did the math for himself. She could wipe the minds of vampires, but not his. He would never forget what he saw.

Nitara was careful to make a note of everything in her surroundings. She calculated the world around her, compiling the factors hoping to figure out one thing. How long would it be until it all went up in smoke? Even those who hung around seemed restless. They were all anxious about something unknown. Nitara had been back for nearly a week, and yet, no one had bothered her with their usual requests.

They didn't ask her to conjure endless rivers of blood or to make the sun magically disappear from the sky, which was one of her top requests. She'd been prepared for the eternal nonsense to kick right back into gear, but still had yet to see much of it.

She wasn't complaining about the lack of being pestered, but it raised some serious red flags for her.

"Sarah," Nitara addressed the vampire who stood on the quiet balcony overlooking Tyrellis' courtyard. "Have you seen him?"

"No, I haven't, not for a few days now, but that isn't exactly unusual. Is there something wrong?" Sarah was a leggy blonde with fair skin and green eyes. Most times she was quiet, demure, but Nitara had seen the darker side of Tyrellis' wife quite a few times. Despite her ability to scare the living hell out of those around her, Sarah was the only thing about the man that made him tolerable.

Where he lacked sensibility, she was the very definition of it. Nothing in excess, nothing that wasn't necessary for her survival. Yes, she enjoyed her position. But unlike her husband, she didn't let it go to her head. Nitara wondered what the hell she saw in the man, besides his power, but Sarah had been with him long before he'd made his bargain with Daegal. Regardless of the reckless decisions he made, she remained by his side.

"No, not at all." Nitara leaned against the banister and gazed out upon the empty grounds below. The air was chilled; the grips of another winter were tightening around the land. "It's just unlike him. Usually I get constant mental updates, wishes, or whatever. The last few days have been quiet."

"I'd think you'd enjoy the peace." Sarah laughed. "It can't be pleasant, having his incessant chatter in your mind."

"Oh, I have." She thought about the sound of his voice that often interrupted her thoughts to leave the ramblings of a vampire in her head. It was weaker, more juvenile, which caused her to believe that Tyrellis intentionally added bass to his voice whenever he spoke. "Best sleep I've gotten in quite some time."

"But I guess it is unusual for him to leave you unbothered." Turning away from the view in front of her, Sarah watched Nitara closely. It was the first time they'd been alone together since the woman had returned. "To be honest, something has had me rather preoccupied. There is much to be done."

"Why is that, if you don't mind my asking?" Nitara didn't know what Sarah was preparing for, but with Tyrellis out of the loop, there were a lot of things she wouldn't know.

"Oh, no, I don't mind. I never do. Not with you." Sarah lifted her hand to secure a loose strand of hair. The woman wasn't one to be seen in a state of unkempt. When the blonde strand was returned to its place, she continued. "Things are changing, Nitara, and I need to find my place in the newly forming world."

"What do you mean?" It wasn't the first time she'd heard that kind of talk, but it was the first time she heard it from Sarah. Usually the woman was so confident. Apparently, something had altered her position on the matter. "You're in the lead of the vampiric race. Why would you ever want to change that?"

"Nitara, while you were away," she paused, weighing her words, "let's just say I did things that I never thought I would. All for the sake of keeping Tyrellis safe, but I fear those things may come back to haunt me."

"Is that right?" Nitara wondered what Sarah had gotten involved in. What could she have done?

"Yes. You know, after such a long time on this unnerving planet, I've learned that not one thing in life will remain the same forever. That is the only thing that is absolutely guaranteed in life. Things will always transform with time. We must adapt, change with the times, or be swept away with the debris of history."

"What did you do?" Nitara knew it was a long shot. If Sarah had done something that she felt could jeopardize her position, she wouldn't be eager to shout it out to the world. Nitara was a direct line to Tyrellis, someone she'd want to keep her dirty little secret from more than anyone else.

"That isn't important now." She avoided the question as expected. "I really like you, Nitara. I always have. You know that, right?"

"Yes, and I like you as well, Sarah." Yeah, Nitara liked Sarah. The woman was a badass and hard not to like, but her little confession of guilt made Nitara question if she should be trusted.

After all, nothing about the vampire royalty's relationship made sense. Sarah was stronger than he was, and yet she ran behind him like a pet. Perhaps she saw his potential or somehow knew about his coming deal with Daegal. Whatever it was, Nitara could see it wasn't genuine affection. She was good at making Tyrellis feel good, and that was all the moron cared about.

"Good. That really makes me happy to know." She looked at the sky, to where they both spotted the wings of a phoenix taking flight. Sarah raised a brow at Nitara who shrugged; that sighting was surely an oddity for Reverie.

Nitara could see the sorrow behind Sarah's eyes. "Are you sure you're okay?"

"I'm perfectly fine, just lost in thought." Sarah's hand brushed across Nitara's shoulder as she turned to leave. "I must go, the sun will be up soon."

"Of course." Watching her leave, Nitara wondered about the ominous meaning behind her words.

"No one must ever know." Spiked heels made sharp snaps as the leggy vampire paced the floor of the simple apartment, careful to stay clear of the windows. If anyone caught even a glimpse of her there, it would ruin everything for her. "I need to be sure that this will stay between the two of us."

"So you said, and I already promised you before that I would keep your secret. Why the reiteration now?" The man watched her and questioned her sudden suspicions.

She was more nervous than he'd ever witnessed her. Her entire body was stiff, rigid with anxiety.

"Yes, but ..." She faced him as her mind raced and turned over the events that took place as she continued to speculate. She tried desperately to find the flaw, the thing that she'd overlooked. There had to be something or else the gnawing pain in her stomach would have subsided. Intuition was working overtime, and it told her she was royally screwed.

"But what? Do you regret telling me? I would think you'd be satisfied ... it saved your husband's life, didn't it? I would think you would be pleased." He stood from the chair, tired of watching her pace, and opted to get himself a drink. Pulling the bottles of blood from the small refrigerator, he offered her one, but she declined.

"When will you do it?" She finally got around to the question that brought her there. Against her better judgement, she had revealed her husband's greatest weakness, and to the enemy. How long would it be before he used that information for his own gains?

"What is it you think I'm planning to do?" Graham straightened as he looked at a woman who was paler than her usual shade of powder white. She truly feared the man. He couldn't blame her. She'd put not only herself, but Tyrellis, in a terrible predicament. The bond between Tyrellis and Nitara had been a well kept secret for many years, but out of fear, she'd given it up.

Sarah had received word that Cass was making his move on the leader. Nitara was missing in action and, as time went on, the belief was that she would never return. Of course, those who would have Tyrellis removed from his position saw this as their time to strike. Out of nothing more than desperation, Sarah appeared in Graham's home. She had seen his affection for Nitara and hoped that her revelation would work to motivate him to prevent Cass from attacking. It did just that.

Instead of taking Tyrellis' life, Cass chose his own survival. There was no way he would go head-to-head with Graham and survive. His token of cooperation was the bike that Nitara had repossessed when she returned.

"I know you've been with Nitara. Twice now I've heard of you two together since her return." She squared her shoulders. "You must be plotting something, conspiring against Tyrellis."

"What exactly would we be plotting?" Nothing had changed about the bond between the vampire and the djinn. If Tyrellis fell, so would she, and Graham would never sign up for that.

"Just tell me what I can do." Sarah suddenly softened; the rigid energy had drained from her body in the blink of an eye as she took a different approach to gaining favor with the opposition. Frantic steps became liquid movements of seduction as she sauntered across the room and over to him. Placing her hand on his chest, she leaned in close to him until her lips were less than an inch away from his ear. "Anything at all. I'll do it for you." Crimson painted lips lowered to the bare flesh of his neck. They brushed against his soft brown skin as she whispered, "Just say the word."

"Sarah," Graham grabbed the hand that started a journey south, and pushed her away, "you are an exquisite woman, but I'm going to have to decline the offer."

"You will need someone by your side." She pouted, and he lost all respect for her.

Yeah, she'd made some poor decisions, especially after confiding in him, but he had respected her. She did what she thought was right. It may have been the wrong thing to do, but she made that choice with good intention. To use her body to entice him, despite her proclamation of love for Tyrellis, it was an all-time low that he never thought he would witness from her.

"Yes, but it won't be you. You who so easily gave up your husband's most precious secret, the thing I could have used to take him out." He placed his drink down and headed for the door. It was time for her to leave. "Why the hell would I want you by my side?"

"I did that to save him." She spoke in hushed anger as she followed him. Still aware of her vulnerability, she wanted no one to know that she was there.

"Did you? Perhaps you tell yourself that to help you sleep at day, but is that the truth? And what about now?" He turned, grabbed her, and pulled her close to him. His waist thrusted against hers and she purred, ready to comply with whatever he demanded of her. "Are you still trying to save him?"

He pushed her through the open door and slammed the door in her face. Her mouth hung open for a moment as the surprise wore off. The sound of movement coming from the far end of the hall snapped her out of it. She kicked the door and grunted. She left in a flash, using her heightened speed before anyone could see her.

CHAPTER 6

Rising Suspicions

"She's going to leave you, you know that." Sarah spoke in a soft whisper against her lover's ear as his lips pressed against his neck. Her fingers combed through blond dyed hair, slick with sweat from the exertion of their lovemaking. She squeezed her thighs around his waist, signaling that she was ready for more of him.

He scoffed, pushing the woman from on top of him. "Must you start in on this now?" The leader of the vampires moved away from her, stood from the bed, and grabbed the thick black robe to cover his body. She pouted as he escaped her hold, but remained in her position, exposed on the bed. The cool air that replaced the heat of his body caused her skin to prickle with goosebumps.

"Yes, I must." She paused before continuing. This hadn't been the first time Sarah would try to convince the man to change his ways and his alliances. The difference was now she had actual proof, evidence to support her claim. "There is nothing to keep her here. Eventually, she will figure out how to get around the magic that binds her to you. What will you do without her? What do you think the others will do when they figure it out?"

"There is nothing she can do about it. She is mine forever. That is what was promised to you." Tyrellis smiled the same greedy grin that always splayed across his face when he considered the gift that was given to him the in form of a full-figured djinn. "The deal ensures it; you know that as well as I do."

"You are quoting the terms of a deal made with a dead man. Can you be sure his magic will hold up? Are you certain of that? Everyone with the sense of a mouse knows that there is a loophole to every spell, a weakness that, once found, can be exploited." Naked, she climbed from the bed.

"You think I should be concerned?" He walked away from her and stared out the window at the black sky that hung above.

"Nitara hasn't been as faithful to you as you would love to believe." Grabbing her own robe, she pulled it tightly around herself and followed him.

"What do you mean? She has reinforced my position." He glanced down at the hand she laid on his shoulder and nodded. "Everything is as it should be."

"Is it really?" Leaving his side, she moved toward the closet where her jacket hung. From inside of the pocket, she retrieved a small envelope and handed it to him. "Has she really done so much to enforce your place here? Or has she made alliances with the enemy?"

"What's this?" He flipped the envelope over and looked at her.

"Open it and find out." Her arms folded across her chest as she waited for him to comply.

Opening the envelope, he found a photograph inside. Shown was Nitara, who sat at the local bar, and she was not alone. "What is this? What am I looking at?"

"That is a photograph of your precious djinn, your ticket to eternal bliss, consorting with a known enemy," Sarah said proudly. Finally, she had solid proof of the very thing she'd been warning him about. The grim expression that briefly flashed across his face was the confirmation she needed. Perhaps now he would consider her warning.

"An enemy?" He peered at the photo again, narrowing his eyes as if it would change the image in front of him. "What the hell are you talking about? This man is no enemy that I know of."

"Yes, he is an enemy! He's one of the biggest threats to your position right now." She scoffed, irritated by her husband's ignorance. "Are you telling me you don't recognize him?"

"That's exactly what I'm telling you." Tyrellis handed the photograph back to his frustrated mate and returned his gaze to the sky. "How big of a threat could he be if I don't recognize his face?"

"It's Graham!" She scowled at the back of his neck. "How could you forget the face of the man you stole your position from? Are you not able to look outside of yourself even for a moment to see the world around you?"

"It doesn't matter." He waved her off. "None of this matters, because as it seems you have forgotten, Nitara is under my control. She couldn't consort with him without my knowing. If there was anything at all to worry about, I would know about it." Even as he spoke the words, he questioned the validity of them. Did he really believe that? Since Nitara's return, she had been more distant than before, more secretive. He'd considered it was his own paranoia, but perhaps he was wrong.

"Oh, and did you know about this, about their other meetings at the local bar? They sit, in public, mocking your position, and yet you think she is on your side," she continued as she closed in on him, her voice lowering to add to the ominous tone of her words. "They leave, moments within one another, and neither are seen nor heard from for hours. What do you suppose they are doing during that time?"

"What would you have me do?" He turned on her, eyes red with fury. It was time for the conversation to end. "Do you believe I should stop her from talking to anyone, from enjoying life? The woman is allowed a personal life." He'd decided long ago to allow Nitara some freedoms, to have her angry at him caused him pain he never spoke of. Daegal was an asshole who not only made it so that she could never leave him, but made it so that he could never abuse her. Apparently, the old bastard still had a soft spot.

"Grow a pair maybe?" She rolled her eyes. "Learn to see what is right in front of you!"

"Watch your mouth." He grabbed her by the throat, and she choked beneath his grip, but held her ground. "Remember who you're talking to! I will take only so much back talk, even from you, my lovely, insatiable wife."

"Look, if you really want to make a point and secure your position, you better stop depending on your rogue pet to do it for you." She spoke through a tight jaw. When his grip relaxed, she softened. "I just want the best for you, as I always have."

"Is that right?" Cocking his head, he peered down his nose and eyed the woman in front of him. Sarah had always been by his side. He could trust her, but then again, he'd felt the same way about Nitara. A truth that was proving to be quite fallible.

"Yes, my love, you know it is." She whispered and ran her hand up his arm.

"Prove it." He dropped his robe, exposing himself beneath the light of the moon, and she fell to her knees in front of him. He groaned as she took him in and offered herself for his taking.

"You called?" Nitara sighed as the smoke cleared from the room. She'd known Tyrellis' silence was too good to continue for long. She'd tried to enjoy every moment, but alas, it was over. Standing in his bedroom that still smelled of the sweaty, bloody sex he'd just had with Sarah, she frowned.

"What is this?" He held out the photograph to her.

Peering at the image, she shrugged. "It looks like a picture of me on patrol, stopping for a drink. Looks fairly obvious. I'm not really sure why you called me here for that."

"Why are you speaking to Graham? And why am I being told that this has become standard practice?" Tyrellis tossed out the veiled accusation.

"I enjoy his sense of humor. Besides, why would I not?" Graham was the only person in Reverie that loathed the place as much as she did—he was also the only one who didn't ask her for bullshit or run terrified whenever she entered the room. "You never told me he was someone I had to avoid. And if you recall, you supplied me with quite a long list when we first came together."

"I allow you the freedom to do as you please, and this is how you repay me?" Tyrellis went on as if she hadn't said a thing. His growing paranoia had him looking at her like she was the enemy he needed protection from.

"Once again, I'm going to tell you I have no idea what you're talking about." She could see it, the wide-eyed look of a man who'd finally snapped. The power had gone to his head and the fear of losing it was making him insane.

"The picture. His hand is in yours. If you were just there to have a drink, why the intimacy?" He'd examined every inch of the photo a thousand times over. The two were being far too familiar with each other for them to be strangers. There was something more there and the idea of it crawled beneath the layers of his skin and turned his stomach sour.

"So, I'm supposed to live here in vampire land for the rest of my existence and never once have a remotely intimate situation with anyone?"

"This is not the time for your sarcasm." Slowly, his fangs fell forward—he would do nothing with them, not that he could do anything to hurt her. It was just for show. This was to let her know he was serious about his suspicions.

"Who said I was being sarcastic? Take a moment to consider how unrealistic you sound right now," Nitara defended herself. "When have I ever done anything to make you think you couldn't trust me?"

"Consider watching your mouth!" he yelled, and pain shot through her. "I own you! Something tells me you've forgotten the dynamics of our arrangement. Perhaps you need a reminder!" He narrowed his gaze and a sharp pain shot through her stomach like bullet wounds.

Doubling over until she fell to her knees, she gripped her sides. "Oh, trust me, I haven't forgotten," she spat at him. "How could I when your incessant whining plays like a soundtrack in my mind!"

"Are you working against me? Tell me! Are you plotting with Graham against my life?" he asked her directly, as if the previous implications weren't clear enough.

"No." She gave her blunt response between labored breaths as the pain subsided.

"I command you to tell me the truth!" He grinned widely; she wouldn't be able to lie to him even if she wanted to. "This is what you warned me of, is it not? That someday others would know and the vampire legions would rise against me. Is life here with me so miserable that you would plot to destroy me, knowing that it would mean ending yourself as well?"

"Tyrellis, my answer remains the same, with or without your command. Besides, why would I waste the effort in lying to you when I know damn well all you have to do is command me to tell you the truth?" Technically speaking, Nitara had told him no lies. She hadn't spoken a word to Graham about standing against the lunatic leader. If Graham knew anything about their bonded lives, he didn't get the information from her.

"Maybe you are telling me the truth," he conceded, but still his suspicious gaze rested on her figure.

"Of course I am. May I leave now? Or do you have any more questions for me?" Nitara wanted out of the room. She could feel his insanity growing, and it worried her. What would it mean for her if he snapped completely? Their lives were tied together. His pain was her own, but what about his mental state? Would it affect her as well?

"No, I think it would be best if you stay close to me for a while." He snapped his fingers. "Yes, I think that is a good idea. You need to stay with me so that I can be sure."

"Planning to torture me some more?" She sighed, tired of him. "I'm not working with any vampire to go against you."

"Good. Nevertheless, I think it's time we put tighter restraints on the amount of freedom I've given you. Some time away from this world might just do you some good." Opening his arms, he bared his chest to her. "Come to me."

"You plan to keep me locked inside forever?" She wouldn't allow it. If she had to erupt a volcano inside of his mind, she would, but he wouldn't keep her banished inside his empty chest.

"No, not forever," he spoke as the magic worked to pull her into him. "But long enough!"

CHAPTER 7

Wake Up Call

*T*he door to the suburban domicile was slightly open, and the foul smell of spilled beer and rotted food reached out to greet her. Inda cautiously approached the entrance to the dark interior. She called a flame to the tip of her finger and used it to light the way as she pushed the door aside and tiptoed through the shadowed hallway into the rank living room.

The smell was so bad she gagged every three steps. She pinched her nose, hoping for relief, but breathing through her mouth didn't work because the air tasted just as bad as it smelled. Stretched across the large sofa and snoring as if he wasn't atop a landfill, was a man who, at the moment, didn't live up to the legend that came with his name.

The wall opposite his strewn form had the only light switch she could see. She sighed. This meant an acrobatic display to get to the switch and avoid stepping into something that would likely cause an infection. She made it across, nearly falling twice and cursing the slumbering man when her boot landed in the center of a large, moldy pizza.

Still she reached her target and turning on the light only made things worse. Inda scoffed at the condition of the place, now completely unhidden. The man was a pig. Speaking of the man, Jinn simply groaned at the disturbance caused by the light, threw his arm over his face, and kept on snoring.

"You've got to be kidding me." Frowning, she stomped over to him. This time kicking the trash as she moved. "Yo!" she yelled, kicked his leg quickly, and then backed away. She was mad, but she wasn't crazy. He was still a powerful ass djinn, and a drunk one by the looks of it. She couldn't be sure the man wouldn't be volatile. The last thing she needed was to have him blow her head off. For all she knew, he would turn shooting out a ball of flames and blow her to bits and pieces. Yes, she was a phoenix, which meant she would be reborn eventually, but she had no intention of going through it, not again. The rebirth thing was handy, but the process was a bitch!

"Jinn! Come on, man, wake up!" Inda yelled at him, only to receive another annoyed grunt from the man who wanted nothing more than to continue sleeping.

When he continued to ignore her request for his conscious attention, she made her way into the kitchen, stumbling over more trash and debris from his apparent pity party, and retrieved a pot out of a cabinet. She then filled that pot with water and carried it back to the disgusting living room. She contemplated calling flames to her fingers to boil the contents, but felt that might be over the top.

"This oughta wake your ass up." Inda smile and flipped the pot over above his head. The water splashed, soaking his face, body, and comfy couch on which he laid. She couldn't help laughing at his erratic movements as it finally pulled him from his drunken dreams.

"What the fuck!" Jinn jumped from the couch. The bottle in his hand fell to the floor, and he glared at the woman in front of her. "Who the fuck are you, and why are you in my house?"

"I'm someone who came to deliver a message to a powerful man but found a bum in his place." She threw the empty pot on the floor. "A friend thinks you want to hear from them, but from the looks of this place, I'm not so sure they're right. Still, I said I would do it, so I will. But I'm going to need you to have some damn manners when talking to me. I didn't sign up for this shit, trust me."

"Damn it. Who the hell would send a phoenix to bother me? If this was Mike, you can fly your ass back to him and tell him I'm going to return the favor with a kick in the ass." He waved his hand, and a towel appeared which he used to dry the water from his face. "Hell, I should have known it. You know, you damn phoenixes have a lot of nerve. Just because you can be reborn doesn't mean I won't just keep killing your ass." The towel turned to a flame of blue light and hovered about his hand.

"Oh, please, spare me." Inda lifted her hand, which was engulfed in its own flame. "We both know that I can do that, too. You wanna cut the act now? It's not really that convincing, considering you can barely stand upright."

"Fuck it! It's not worth it!" He dropped his hand, and the flame went out. She was right—not only was he shaky on his feet, but he just didn't care enough to really be upset about her intrusion. The best bet was to deal with her and send the woman on her way. "Are you going to tell me what you want, or do I have to pull it out of you?" He conjured another bottle of whiskey to replace the one that had spilled during his startling wake-up call.

"Like I said before, I'm here with a message from a friend. I think it would be best if you weren't pissed off your ass when I gave it to you." She frowned as he finished the bottle and dropped it on the growing pile of trash at his feet. "Maybe you can clean yourself up a bit?"

"Well, if that's what you want, you're going to be here for a long goddamn time." Jinn had no interest in tidying up for the woman. If she had a message to deliver, she could do so and fly her pretty little ass back to wherever she came from. Demanding that he do anything for the sake of her pleasure was a bad move. Information she didn't deliver was information he never had, and either way, it didn't matter to him.

Inda sucked her teeth, irritated that he wouldn't budge. "Fine, let's just get this over with. Besides, I'm sick of your smell."

"Oh, I'm sorry to have offended you after you so uninvitedly waltzed into my home and interrupted my nap!" Jinn yelled and the walls shook

"Look, I'm here trying to do you a favor, so you might want to curb the attitude." Inda snipped back, unphased by his outburst.

"Okay, I'm the one with the attitude." He laughed. Every second with the woman only justified his decision to stay away from the world. "How long are we going to do this?"

"Oh, I think just about until you're sober enough to understand me. I would hate to have to repeat myself."

"Oh, for fuck's sake!" he yelled and ran his hands through his hair, which had grown drastically since his last cut. "Why don't you just make yourself at home, then? I'm going to go take a shower. Perhaps when I get back, you'll feel more comfortable telling me whatever the hell you were sent here to say."

The shower did Jinn a lot of good. Despite his desire to stay shitfaced, his mind cleared right along with the smell of the countless beers and bourbon he'd consumed. Once again, the outside world insisted that he return from his self-inflicted exile. What the hell did he have to look forward to outside of the four walls surrounding him? He'd been dumped on his ass, and after going to the end of the world to save the woman he'd wasted centuries loving. Not only that, but while consumed with saving her, he'd lost the only other person he cared about.

No one had seen or heard from Praia since she'd risked her life to save the world. The ocean swallowed her up. He hadn't even known. It wasn't until after Nitara walked out on him that he looked for her. Mike, the asshole who started it all with a stupid ass picture that no one needed to see, was supposed to find her. He returned empty-handed. Jinn spent two weeks searching, only to find no trace of the girl who'd latched on to him and never let go.

He touched the charm that still hung around his neck. It'd been months, but he still hoped that it would someday light up and she would return to his life. One day she would be back in his home, hogging his couch, and demanding magically made steaks. He shook the thought of the fae girl from his mind, along with everyone else tied to her disappearance.

His frowning guest met Jinn when he emerged from his bedroom wearing nothing but a pair of grey sweatpants and a towel hanging around his neck. His skin was still wet from the shower, the air felt good to him. She'd created one clean spot on the couch where she sat with an expression of disgust on her face. Already sensing the tongue lashing she was prepared to give him; he snapped his fingers. What was once a pigsty became a freshly cleaned home. "There, you happy?"

"You say that as if you've done me a favor." Inda rolled her eyes at the man who strutted across the room. "I should be asking you that. I didn't know you liked to live in such conditions. The way people talk about you, that should be the first bullet point. Powerful djinn, and pig!"

"Bite me," he groaned.

"I would, but I don't eat swine." She stuck her tongue out as he flipped her off and headed for the kitchen. When he returned, he had a full beer in one hand and a sandwich in the other. Of course, he offered her nothing.

"What do you want?" he questioned through a mouthful of food. "I'd like to get this over with so I can get back to my nap!"

"I guess direct it is, then." Rising from the sofa, she squared off with him. "I have a message from Reverie."

"Reverie?" He scoffed; he had no vampire friends. Who the hell could be looking to reach him? "What could anyone in vamp land have to say to me?"

"It would seem there is someone there who needs your help. Someone who we all know you will want to drag your ass out of this dump and save." Inda teased with the first bit of information.

"And that is?" He waved his hand for her to continue. "I don't have all day for this."

"Oh, and what else were you going to do besides conjure another pizza for you not to eat?" She scoffed.

"I'm warning you, woman. Say what you have to say or go." He lifted a finger, and Inda felt a force pressing against her chest. Her feet slid across the hardwood floors as he pushed her toward the exit.

"Fine, okay!" The pressure stopped, and she straightened herself. "It's Nitara. She needs your help ... again."

Jinn's jaw tightened as he processed what she said to him. "Get out," he ordered the woman, who stared at him in disbelief. "Sprout your wings and fly the hell away from my home."

"What?" Inda's mouth fell open. She hadn't been expecting a no from him. Everyone thought he would be eager to put his life on the line again for the woman he loved. They were all wrong.

"You heard me. Get the hell out!" He yelled and this time, the entire house shook. The floor rumbled beneath her feet and the blue flame highlighted his entire body.

"You have got to be kidding me! I did not fly all the way down here for you to kick me out."

"Well, I suggest you find something else to do with your time." Jinn waved his hand and forced the bird of fire down the hall and out the door. Before she could protest or spout off another one of her witty remarks about him or the state of his home, the door slammed in her face.

Inda fought with the handle and banged her fist on the door, but to no avail. "Oh, fuck!"

CHAPTER 8

Old Friends

Inda flew above the fairy city, confident that her relationship with their new queen would give her a pass. Usually, the fairies would stop anyone who dared to enter their city either by air or ground. She hoped her name was on a special list. Briar should have been expecting her, anyway. As she assumed, she flew right on in. After one encounter with a guard verifying who she was, no one else bothered her. Below her, she could see the lively fairies as they moved throughout the city. It was odd how ordinary their lives looked.

They went about shopping, working, and having small talk as they walked their dogs. If she hadn't known better, she'd imagine it was just another human city. Of course, the buildings that sprouted from the ground and the wildlife strolling through the streets also debunked that theory. She took her time about reaching her destination. Word would have gotten to Briar about the visitor she wouldn't be expecting. She gave her friend a little time to get herself together.

"Inda, it's good to see you." The woman who met her reminded her so much of her friend. It was as if she was a replication. Same hairstyle, pulled back into a bun, and her uniform was clean, pressed, not a stitch out of place. Briar had really made her mark, not only as their leader, but apparently as a fashion icon. Inda wondered what the new queen looked like. Did she keep her own style or conform to the standard set by those previously in her role?

"You as well. You're looking mighty fine." She said playfully and smiled at Mysti. She hadn't seen the woman who was now second in command to her best friend in a long time, but she was never one to forget a face. "Tell me something. Do you think my dear old friend could take a bite out of what I'm sure is a busy scheduled to see a tired bird? It was a long flight in."

"For you, of course. Hang tight." Mysti left Inda in the lobby of the city's center where the queen lived. She headed off to get things in order for her visit. There was no way Briar would turn her away, not after how long it had been since the two hung out. Besides, the two had a lot to discuss.

Sitting in the lush waiting area, Inda made note of the changes that her friend had apparently implemented. The large pane windows covering the building from top to bottom had been reinforced. She could see the signature of the magic that was used to further secure the building. After what happened to the last queen, and the infiltration that went unnoticed, it was no wonder she would want more security.

The step up in safety wasn't the only thing that changed. There were a lot of unfamiliar faces, faces that at one point, she wouldn't have assumed belonged in Vilar. Fae, the magical beings of the moon, were there. In the past, the two species stayed away from each other. Fairies were of the sun and the fae of the moon. The two celestial beings never shared the sky, and their children avoided each other just as adamantly.

"Inda, she is ready for you." Mysti returned and motioned for the visitor to follow her. They climbed the staircase, which led to the only elevator that would take them to the queen's chamber. Inda had never been past the main entrance to the building. The few times she had visited Briar, her friend had met her at the door and quickly escorted her far away from the glistening fairy palace.

Inda had to contain her excitement as the elevator reached the top level and the doors slid open. On the other side was a small waiting area where guests would stay until the queen was ready for them. They did the floors in a gorgeous red carpet that looked as if it were lit with flames. It matched the new queen who had an affinity for fire. The gold double doors opened as they stepped out of the elevator to reveal the chamber behind them. A large room with beautifully painted walls and jeweled accents was where the throne sat, empty. Inda took in the sight of it all and couldn't believe that this was her friend's new life.

"The Queen will be with you in a moment." Mysti announced. "You can wait here for her."

Mysti left Inda in the room alone. There she stood, waiting and making mental photographs of every detail of the space, until a voice she hadn't heard in far too long interrupted her thoughts.

"Inda!" Briar burst into the room from a door behind the throne. She smiled brighter than she ever had before when she saw Inda there. In part, she'd thought that someone was playing a cruel joke on her, falsely announcing the arrival of her long-lost friend. She was happy to find that she'd been worried for nothing. "It's so good to see you."

"You too!" Inda couldn't believe her eyes. In all of their time as friends, she had never seen Briar in anything but jeans, boots, and a leather jacket. Of course, her attire became more uniformed when she joined the fairy guard, but it was nothing like what she was seeing now. Her friend comfortably modeled a long, flowing dress with lace that hung from her shoulder, mimicking the wings that would carry her should she choose to take flight.

"Are you sure about that?" Briar asked hesitantly. She wanted to pull her friend into a tight hug, but she refrained from the action. Inda had yet to forgive her for betraying her trust and she couldn't presume that her arrival meant that she had a sudden change of heart. For all she knew, the phoenix was there to deliver the ass kicking she promised to give her if Briar failed to keep her secret.

"Yes, despite your terrible betrayal," Inda teased her friend, who immediately blushed with apology.

"I'm sorry, but I had to. You know there is no way I would have told Jax anything if I could have seen there being any other way to convince him to help us." Straight to the point, that was Inda's way. Though she teased, Briar knew that she had really hurt her friend when she gave up her secret. She wanted so much to ask her if she had spoken to Jax, but it wasn't the time. If they were truly going to make amends, there would be an opportunity to speak about everything later.

"I know that." Inda couldn't help it; she'd already forgiven Briar, though she wanted to be mad. She couldn't. They wouldn't be friends if she thought the woman was capable of any malice toward her. "I mean, it really sucked, and it may have taken me some time to come to terms with it, but I know you wouldn't do anything to hurt me, not unless it was a last resort. And even then, you're great at begging for forgiveness."

"So, you forgive me? I sent gifts, cards, and letters, but heard nothing back. Figured you burned them all." Briar really had gone above and beyond—she sent gift after gift, and hoped for a response that never came, even with confirmation that the gifts were delivered.

"You know I do." Inda sighed. "I'm a fool, and I cannot stay mad at you."

"Great!" Briar pulled Inda into another warm hug, this one heated even more so by her increased happiness. "So, what brings you here, or was it just to hear me plead for your forgiveness in person?"

"I wouldn't call what you just did pleading, but yes, I must admit that I came here with another agenda." She sighed. "Not that reconnecting with you isn't great, but there are other things that I have to take care of while I'm here. Unfortunately, it's not nearly as easy I as assumed it would be."

"What do you have to do?" Briar ushered her over to the sitting area where tea and pastries awaited them. "Maybe I can help?"

"Black and white cookies, my favorite! You remembered!" Inda squealed as she quickly stuffed one of the soft cake-like cookies into her mouth. "Oh, they are just as good as I remember!"

"I'm glad. I had the kitchen make them especially for you, and there is a box of them waiting for you to take home."

"You're the best friend a girl could ever ask for!" Inda grabbed another cookie, though she hadn't finished the one already in her mouth.

"I try." Briar sipped from her teacup. "So, tell me, what is the problem you're facing? We can figure it out together. Like old time. You know, I'm not sure if you noticed, but I kind of run things around here now."

"Yes, I noticed! And you look amazing." She slapped her leg and leaned back in her chair. "I mean, look at you! You're in a dress!"

"I know. I never thought I'd be this comfortable in one, but if I'm honest, they've grown on me." Briar glowed with joy. "Anyway, we can discuss all of that later. What's your problem? I want to help."

"My problem is a drunken asshole who goes by the name of Jinn." Inda huffed.

"Jinn?" Briar frowned. "What do you want with him?"

"Oh, you know, same old story." She popped another cookie into her mouth and followed it with a swig of tea. "A bunch of us need his help in a plot to save his long-lost love."

"What?" Briar placed her cup back on the table. "You're plotting to do what?"

"I know. It must sound like a broken record to you." She polished off the last two cookies and looked for more. Flying with wings of fire burned a lot of calories. She would have preferred something high in protein, but the cookies were hitting the spot. "Nitara, she needs him. Call me a feminist or whatever, but this woman always needing him to come save her is getting tired."

"I'm sure it's more complicated than that." Briar laughed. "If I were you, I wouldn't rush to bring that topic up to him. It's a bit of a sore spot with him after the way their last encounter ended."

"Yeah. That would have been nice to know before I went knocking on his funky ass door." Her attempt to confront the problem head-on had backfired and left her with a door slammed in her face. She hadn't even wanted to be involved, but she gave her word and wouldn't walk away until she convinced the man to get off his ass and help his wife. "This was supposed to be a simple job."

"Oh, you already visited him." Briar couldn't help the smirk. She thought of the last person to visit Jinn. It was a mission that proved to be quite comical for everyone who warned the dragon not to go there. Rick, one of the dragons who helped them fight Daegal and save the world, had demanded that Jinn step up and help find Praia. He pounded down the door, though everyone warned him against it. If it wasn't for Jax stepping in, Rick would have lost his life that day.

"Yes, I did. You want to know what I received for my efforts to help? A swift kick in the ass that left me standing on his stoop with egg on my face! As happy as I am to see you and to squash this tension between us, that is why I'm here now."

"You think I can get through to him?" It made sense. After all, they had worked side by side to save the world. The assumption was a sound one, but it was also incorrect. She had been no more successful at breaking through to the man than anyone else had. Yeah, she tried a few times, but each time she hadn't gotten past the threshold. At least Inda made it inside.

"Yes, well, I hope you can." She popped another cookie into her mouth. "If not, I flew my pretty ass down here for nothing."

"Understand something here. Nitara really broke Jinn's heart." Briar said. "Inda, this wasn't some simple break up. She crushed him when she left."

"Yeah, I know. What I came down here to tell the jerk was that she only did it because she felt she didn't have a choice in the matter." Inda rolled her eyes. "Of course he didn't give me a chance to say all that now, did he?"

"I highly doubt that I can convince him of anything," pausing, Briar touched her chin with her finger, "but I know someone who might."

"Well, whoever it is, bring their ass on. I would like to get this over with." Inda groaned. "I got other shit to do."

Briar considered her next question carefully before she asked it. They would have to talk about it at some point. Why not bring it up while she was happily stuffing her face with cookies? "Have you talked to him?"

"No, and I don't plan on it." Inda straightened in her seat. Her head tilted to the side, and she narrowed her gaze at the woman who sat across from her. "Should he just happen to stop by while I'm here, I'll know who to blame."

"Hey, I've learned my lesson. My lips are sealed!" Briar lifted her hands in surrender.

"Sure they are." She laughed. "So, can I get room and board for the night?"

"Of course!" Briar clapped her hands. "You shall have our very best accommodations!"

"And that includes food, correct?" Inda rubbed her stomach and groaned. "Love the cookies, but I need some real fuel for my engine!"

"Yes, as much as your heart desires!" Briar laughed at her friend, who was still as hilarious and sassy as she remembered her to be.

"I knew there was a reason you're my best friend!"

CHAPTER 9

Reinforcements

"I *hope the accommodations were to your liking."* Briar smiled as Inda flowed into the room wearing a dress designed specifically for her. It was a gift delivered to her room that morning. It fit her perfectly.

"Yes! You know, that was the best night of sleep I've had in a very long time." She beamed. "I felt like I was sleeping on a cloud!"

"Good. I'm happy to hear that." Briar raised a brow. "I already know you ate well, based on the reports from the kitchen." She snickered, happy to tease the woman, who showed no remorse for the reports of her gluttony. According to the kitchen staff, Inda had given them a run for their money. There were jokes about needing to restock the pantry after finally satisfying her appetite.

"Hey, you told me to make myself at home!" Inda laughed and twirled in the red dress they gave her. The design made her feel like she was a fairy. She would have to remember not to shift or the lacey material would go up in flames. As much as she liked it, she would hate to see it reduced to a pile of ash. "Thanks for the new threads, by the way."

"Well, we're expecting a bit of royalty to arrive soon. If you're to be a part of the welcoming party, you'll need to look the part." Briar was also dressed in her best. She wore a design similar to the one she'd had on the day before, only now she was adorned in jewels.

"Your life is so different now." Inda shook her head in continued disbelief. "I would have never imagined you like this. I have to admit, I like it. You're stunning!"

"Thanks, Indy." Briar carefully hugged her friend. "I guess becoming the queen has that effect. Trust me, it wasn't a simple transition, but I have to admit, it has grown on me. Besides, I can wear whatever I want. Most days, unless something special is happening, I'm still in jeans and combat boots!"

"I take it that means my arrival was special?" Inda poked, reminding Briar of the attire she wore when her friend had arrived.

"Absolutely!" she exclaimed and laughed. "Besides, I couldn't miss the opportunity to see that look of shock on your face."

"Damn near knocked me on my ass to see anything but boots on your feet. So, no more late nights drinking and scoping out guys at the bar?" Inda thought back to their past. Before the world changed, the two of them share a lot of wild nights together. No man was safe. At least no man with a pair of soulful eyes and a tight ass!

"I didn't really like all that anyway," Briar lied.

"Yeah, sure ... whatever you say." Inda laughed. Briar always kept a tough exterior, but when it was just the two of them, she let that guard down. No one in the world could see her the way Inda did.

"Our guests have arrived at the borders." Boxi, another fairy guard, peeked through the door to announce the help Briar had called for. "They'll be here soon."

"Great, thank you. We should meet them. Let's make sure everything is in order. Double check the security. I'm not expecting any trouble, but you can never be too sure." Boxi nodded and left the room to do as she was told. Briar gestured to Inda. "After you."

"Oh, no, after you." Inda bowed. Friends or not, Briar was queen and there were protocols that had to be met.

"The bow really isn't necessary." Briar scoffed.

"But tell me it didn't make you feel good!" she squealed, and the two headed for the exit giggling like little girls.

The precession was less magnificent than Inda expected it to be, considering it was a royal family arriving. There were just a few trucks that drove down the city streets. Six in all, black SUVs that reminded her of a scene from a movie she once saw. Inside there were only a few guards and a king. When they filed out of their vehicles, Inda had to hold back the gasp. No one had prepared her for what she saw.

In front of Vilar, Briar and her guards greeted the King of the Slithers. The slithers were reptilian shifters, the product of magical experiments gone wrong. They were cast to the outskirts and made to dwell in uninhabitable lands after they failed to take a side and stick to it during the war. Playing on both sides of the fence was a risky thing, and it didn't play out in their favor. Mike, the leader of his people, was the one who fought for the improvement of their standard of life. If it weren't for his deal with Briar, the slithers would still be a group unaccepted by the rest of civilization. Inda had never actually seen a slither up close and personal. She looked at them with the same wonderment that she received. While a few could pass for human, others had scales on their skin and features that were permanently reptilian.

"Mike, it's good to see you again," Briar greeted the man who had his own guards by his side. She held out her gloved hand to him and he kissed the back of it. They were good at keeping up the formalities. "I'm so glad you could come on such short notice."

"Well, of course, it's not often you ask anything of me. I figure it must be important. Besides," he looked over his shoulder to the woman holding an infant in her arms, and signaled for her to approach, "you still haven't met my daughter."

"Oh, I hadn't heard your wife had given birth!" Briar looked over her shoulder at Mysti, who shrugged. They'd received no news of the birth. "Did you not make an announcement?"

"I did, but it was a small one. The missus wanted to keep it to herself for a bit. Enjoy the bond before the world dug its claws in." Mike took the bundle of joy from her mother and handed her over to Briar. "She's just a few weeks old now, but she's growing so fast."

"I completely understand the desire to keep your child to yourself. We wait months before introducing new life to the rest of our people. It allows them time to bond with the mother." Briar comfortably cradled the baby in her arms as if it were second nature. Wide, slit eyes looked up at her before the baby cooed and smiled. She shut her eyes and opened them again to reveal a normal pair of green irises. "She is absolutely stunning, Mike. What's her name?"

"Tilia. She's named after the lime trees that are now growing outside of our home, thanks to you." The man couldn't contain his pride as he looked on at his daughter. She would know a better life than he did, and it was because of him. What more could a father hope for?

"That's a beautiful name." Briar returned her focus to the baby girl who gripped her finger. "Hello, Tilia. It's so good to meet you."

"Yes, it matches her. I often find her in her bassinet staring out of the window at the trees. I only wish I could know what she's thinking." Feeling the heated glare of his wife burning into his neck, Mike retrieved the child from Briar and returned her to her mother. "So, why are we here?"

"Perhaps this is the time we move this conversation to a venue that allows for more privacy?" Briar nodded, and her eyes swept across the mixed crowd surrounding them.

"Ah, a call for concealment! That means trouble," Mike joked.

"I didn't know you were one to be afraid of a little trouble," Briar teased as she turned away from him to lead the way.

"Oh, I'm not. Bring it on!" Mike laughed and followed her lead.

"Well, now that we're all settled in, let's get down to business." Briar gestured to the woman who had not yet been introduced. "Mike, I would like you to meet a very close friend of mine. Inda."

"Inda, why does that name sound so familiar?" He scratched his chin and squinted as if that would bring familiarity to the face of the woman he'd never seen before.

"Perhaps you know my ex, the dragon, Prince Jax?" Inda rolled her eyes. Of course, that was the connection he was struggling to make. It was the only reason anyone ever seemed to recognize her name.

"Ah, yes. You're the spitfire giving him the eternal slip!" Mike couldn't help himself. He laughed as he recalled the puppy dog look Jax got whenever Inda's name came up in conversation. "He's got it real bad for you!"

"Yes, that would be me." She ignored his comment about Jax's lingering emotions. "It's nice to meet you."

"You as well. Now, tell me, why are we here? I gotta tell ya, the wife wasn't all that thrilled to make the trip." Kristen, his wife, had been taken to a nursery with their daughter where she could have privacy for herself and the child. She didn't want to be there, but Mike convinced her to tag along. He didn't think it would look right. They were newly reestablished as acceptable members of society. He wanted nothing to jeopardize that. If he'd known about how the fairies felt about concealing children after childbirth, he wouldn't have pressed the issue. It would have definitely saved him a headache.

"I'm sure in time, she and the others will grow more comfortable with things." Briar smiled, but she was unsure. He wasn't the only one getting resistance from his people. Though some fairies were open, and most couldn't care one way or another, there were a few who rebelled against the idea of the slithers being forgiven.

"Yes, I sure hope so. I got a real earful the entire trip." He wished he were joking, but Kristen didn't trust Briar or her people despite all that they had done to help them rebuild and repair their homes.

"Well, prepare for more. What I brought you here for looks to be a start to another one of the mission impossible journeys." Briar could give up on the idea of becoming friends with the Slither Queen any time soon.

"Okay," he leaned back in his chair, "lay it on me."

"Inda is here from Reverie, with a message for our good friend, Jinn. It's regarding the recently departed Nitara." Cut to the chase. Briar had a distinct talent for relaying information in a way that felt like a gut punch.

"You've got to be kidding me." Mike laughed. "How are we here again?" Mike turned his attention to Inda, who shrugged.

"I'm just the messenger. Unfortunately, I gave my word that I would do whatever it took to bring the man back to vamp land to help. Of course, I did not know it would take this much effort after all the stories of their last adventure together. I figured he would be happy for the chance to save the woman again."

"Yes, unfortunately, Jinn risked everything for Nitara, and she dropped him like yesterday's news. Hell, she barely thanked him for what he did for her." Mike straightened. "I'm not sure I care to help the woman after all that."

"Well, it would seem she had no choice in the matter." Inda was skeptical about saying what she needed to, but if they were anything like Jinn in his resistance, she wouldn't have a choice. Ardyn told her to only reveal the information if necessary, and it was definitely necessary. Mike would not budge on the topic without more convincing.

"How so?" He raised a brow as his gaze shifted between the two women.

"Nitara is bonded to a vampire. He is her vessel now, a lovely little trick of whoever the asshole was who made her a djinn. When he died, the spell made sure Nitara still wouldn't be free. Ownership, as it were, went back to Tyrellis. He's the current vampire leader, thanks to his unlimited access to Nitara's power. I know it looks messed up that she left, but she couldn't have stayed here even if she wanted to."

"Well, fuck." Mike had no desire to be involved with the affairs of djinns again, but if what Inda said was true, he had to at least try. Jinn had done so much for them; he'd helped them all find a happier time. Hell, the man helped the entire world. It didn't seem right that he was the only one living in misery.

"You think that will be enough to convince him?" Briar was skeptical and for good reason. It might get Jinn to listen, but it wouldn't be enough. Not without evidence.

"I doubt it. We'll need a lot more than her word to do the trick." Mike rubbed his hand over his chin.

"What are you thinking?" The queen was open to suggestions. She, too, felt the same about the man who'd aided them in saving her race. He was alone and unhappy, and it didn't seem right.

"I'm thinking about a little witch lady who sees the future." Mike tapped his finger on the table. "If it weren't for her, we wouldn't have convinced him the first time around."

"You mean Sybella?" Briar paused and thought about the eccentric Seer who'd suffered greatly with the attack on Alesea, the former queen and her close friend. "I'm not sure she would be up to it after everything that happened. She's still in recovery. As it is, we haven't asked much of her since the incident."

"Well, without her showing him that it is the truth, how do you suppose we get the message across?"

Briar pressed the button on the arm of her chair to alert the guard that stood outside of the doors. Boxi, the large wall of a woman who guarded Briar at all times, stepped into the room.

"Yes, Your Majesty. How can I assist you?" Boxi nodded to Mike quickly before waiting for her orders.

"Get Mysti. Have her go to Sybella's quarters to assess her conditions." Briar instructed. "I will require her to take a trip, and it may be strenuous."

"Yes, right away." Boxi turned to leave, but paused, lifting her finger to her ear. "I'm sorry. It seems your presence is needed. We have an unexpected guest."

"Is that so?" Briar stood from the table. "You two continue without me. Duty calls."

"Mike, I hope you don't mind my asking, but how is it that you are so close with Briar now? I thought the slithers had an aversion to the fairies, and everyone else, for that matter." Inda figured she could dig in and find out a bit more about their supposed ally. She hadn't bothered with the details of what happened once she found out Briar gave up her secret, but Mike was someone who'd been mentioned as a key figure in all that took place.

"It turns out not all of us are like our predecessors." He shrugged; it was something he was used to. Slithers were made out to be horrible people who did shitty things to get what they wanted. The sins of a few disgraced them all. "Same thing goes for Briar."

"Is that so?" Inda raised a brow. "Do you see something different in her?"

"She was able to see outside of what was told of us and to recognize that not all of us are monsters deserving of a life in the swallows. We worked together once we got over our aversion to one another, as you put it."

"And now you're friends." The concept was one that shocked her. Had she been away that long? Briar wasn't one who easily adapted to change. It was so out of character for her, but she had to admit, when she left, Briar had just joined the guard when Alesea begged her to. Hell, the woman barely spoke to most of the fairies. Now she was their leader. They had so much to catch up on, but she doubted the queen would ever have that kind of free time on her hands again.

"Something like that, yes." It wasn't as if they were braiding each other's hair and singing songs. The two had a shared respect and their values and goals aligned. The world needed the peace it was promised when humans were put out of command. Mike, more than anyone, wanted to achieve that. In his short time working alongside Briar, they'd made great strides in that direction.

"What about everyone else?" Inda walked to the bar on the side of the room and grabbed a drink. "It doesn't seem like the rest of your people are on board. Hell, even some of the fairies are averse to the chance."

"They will get there in time." Mike nodded at the bottle she chose, and Inda poured him a drink as well. "No one likes when change happens. Not at first. It's scary, it shakes the faith. Change means pushing someone out of their comfort zone. In this case, it's a good push for my people and even so, they are skeptical. A lot of them are highly reluctant. In time, they will see that it's all for the better. There isn't a trick to it."

"How can you be so confident about that?" She didn't think her friend would do anything backhanded. Briar had always been an honest person, but a lot of things had changed about the woman. She couldn't be sure that her values hadn't transformed as well. Power had a way of going to a person's head. She'd seen it before.

"I have to be. Hell, if I didn't have confidence in the impossible, we wouldn't be here today." Mike had put so much on the line, and at a sensitive time for his growing family. It was part of the reason his wife gave him so much shit. He'd nearly missed the birth of his own daughter because he was out trying to save the world.

"I suppose you're right." Inda sipped her drink and considered how far she was willing to go for a world that really wasn't her own.

The door opened to a flustered Briar who, for a moment, looked like her world had imploded. Mike and Inda exchanged a quick glance, but neither asked her about it. "I'm so sorry about that, just had to deal with a little bug." She eyed the drinks the two were sharing and poured herself a glass. It seemed fitting for the occasion.

A moment later, the door opened again and Mysti, her second in command and the seer who'd they hoped could convince Jinn to help, entered the room.

"Sybella, it's so good to see you again." Mike stood from his seat and approached the small woman. "How are you?"

"I'm well enough to help try to knock some sense into my stubborn old friend." Always the one to keep with traditions, she bowed to both Mike and Briar. "Inda, it's nice to see you here." Of course, no introductions were necessary. She'd known the bird would fly in long before her hot feet touched the ground.

"Thank you again for doing this." Briar sat her drink down. "I know this is difficult for you."

"Yes, well, life must go on." She still mourned the loss of her friend, but her physical wounds had healed with the help of both witch and fairy magic. Her body was whole, even if her heart was not.

"That it must." She nodded. "Still, thank you for this. We all realize that dealing with Jinn can be challenging, but you seemed to have mastered the navigations."

"We'll see about that." She chuckled. "Do you all have a strategy in mind, or will you just be dropping me off at the front door and hoping for a good outcome?"

"That sounds like a plan." Mike clapped his hands. "I'm sure you can take anything that the old fool has to dish out."

Sybella looked at Mike and rolled her eyes. "I vote we drop you off there. You've already taken a blow or two from the man."

Mike laughed. "Hey, I'm resilient. I can take a little heat!"

"Good, because you may have to," Briar interjected.

"Oh?" Mike turned to her. His joke wasn't meant to be taken seriously.

"I think it would be best if you went in first." Briar sipped from her drink.

"Right." He chewed his bottom lip as he thought it over. "Why is that?"

"You have a way of getting through to him. If you can convince him to listen, then we can bring in Sybella. Her going in there won't do much good if she can't get close to him. You have a way of making Jinn do things he wouldn't. Convince him that this is something worth his time, and then Sybella will provide the proof of that."

"What you're telling me is that I get to be the sacrificial lamb, huh?"

"It would appear so." Inda laughed and polished off her drink. "Hey, you're a king. That will count for something."

"It never did before." Mike shook his head. "Technically speaking, I've been a king for as long as I've known Jinn. You think that ever stopped him from ripping me a new one?"

"Judging from how he treated me, I'm going to assume the answer is no." Inda had experienced her own run-in with the man who was the topic and was glad that she wasn't being put in place to take the lead.

"Yeah, well, I'll need a hell of a large drink for this." Mike frowned at the half empty glass in front of him. "When do we do this?"

"How about now? The sooner the better. I need to get back to my life," Inda stated. Truth was she wanted to get away from Vilar just in case Jax showed up. Even if Briar didn't say anything, she couldn't be sure word of her arrival hadn't already made it back to the Cascades. If it had, he'd be on his way there.

"I better go ahead and let Kristen know." Mike exited the room and prepared himself for another tongue lashing from the wife. Being king had its perks, but it did nothing to stop normal marital issues.

CHAPTER 10

He's Alive!

"We better prepare, as well." Briar turned to Mysti as they were left alone. "Get the guards together. Tell them to prepare for a trip. Get Sybella whatever she needs as well."

"Yes, Your Majesty." Mysti ushered Sybella out of the room, leaving Inda along with the queen.

"Does that get weird?" Inda frowned at the woman walking out of the room.

"What?" Briar paused to look at her friend.

"Everyone calling you, 'your majesty'."

"It was at first, but now it's not so bad." She shrugged. It wasn't immediately that she was called by the proper terms, and that was by her request. Things had to return to normal, and that meant being called by her title. She wasn't a fan of it, but she didn't hate it either. "It's really no different from being the head of the guard. Everyone held me in a similar regard as they do now."

"Should I be calling you that?" Inda blushed. Not once since she had arrived had she considered just how much things had changed between her and her friend. Yeah, there were little details like her attire and her fancy new office, but Briar was a queen, the head of her people, and that put her on another level entirely.

"No, please don't." Briar laughed. "That would be weird. You're my friend and people may not like it, but hell, I'm the queen!" She straightened her shoulders and puffed out her chest, and they both giggled.

"Okay, great. So, what should I be doing?" Inda didn't want to be on the front line, but she still wanted to be useful.

"You should be trying not to kill your best friend." Briar had an awkward expression on her face. The same expression she wore whenever she did something she knew Inda would want to flame up about.

"Why would I want to do that?" Frowning, she crossed her arms over her chest. "What did you do?"

"I didn't do anything, but I just got word about a little bug that flew in ..." Briar chewed her lip waiting for Inda's response.

"Jax?" The woman was pacing the floor.

"Yes."

"Fuck, how did he get here so fast?" She peered out the window as if she would be able to see him.

"Apparently, he was nearby." Briar shrugged. "I swear, I have nothing to do with this."

"I believe you. Shit, I knew this would happen the second I got here." She stopped in front of Briar; the pacing hadn't helped to calm her down. "He knows I'm here."

"Yes, and he said he isn't leaving until he sees you." Briar relayed the message to her worried friend.

"Great! I don't want to deal with him, Briar." Inda looked at her friend with eyes that carried so much more than the anger she showed to the world. She was afraid to see her ex. She was afraid of what that reunion would look like, and what it would do to her.

"I realize that. So, I instructed the others to keep him distracted while we sneak out through the secret passage. Boxi will meet us at the exit."

"Thank you." Inda took a deep breath, happy for the escape route.

"This isn't going away, you know. He will still be here when we get back and he knows that you came from Reverie now, so even if you dodge him, he'll just go there."

"Fuck." She was right. Inda had nowhere to go. Jax was on her trail now and he wouldn't stop chasing her.

"Would it be so bad to just talk to him?" Briar led Inda to the back of the room, where a small hidden door blended into the panels. She placed her hand on the surface and her magic unlocked the hatch that held it in place.

"What exactly am I supposed to say? We fought, I left, I'm back, but nothing has changed. That man is an egotistical asshole! He expected me to turn my back on my people for him! I couldn't do that then, and I can't now. If something should happen and I'm called away again ..." She choked on her words and the tears she fought to hold back.

"Is that why you haven't reached out? You're afraid you'll have to leave him again?"

"Yeah, that's a big part of it."

"If that is the case, why did you return here? I mean, there are so many other realms and worlds that you told me about. So many places for you to explore. Why come here if you're afraid of what it means to be here?"

"I don't know. It feels good, though, just knowing he is in the same world, even if we can't be together."

"You may not want my opinion here, but I am going to give it. You've already wasted so much time apart. Perhaps you can put your fears aside and go to him. Even if it doesn't last forever, share that time together, cherish it because you never know when it will be ripped away for good."

"Are you speaking from experience here?" Inda narrowed her gaze. "Is there something you want to tell me about? Or someone?"

"Look at that," Briar snapped her fingers and looked at her bare wrist, "it's time to go!"

"Avoidance, classic." Inda wiped her face of the tear that had escaped and smiled at her friend who ushered her through the hidden door.

"Yes, you should know!" Briar pulled the door shut behind her.

Mike stood outside of Jinn's home as he continued his internal debate. It was hard to walk away from his wife and daughter knowing that if Jinn agreed, it would mean that Mike would be away from them for a lot longer. There was only one way that he could think of to convince the man to step up, and that meant not only one, but two journeys for them to partake in. *Great*.

"Jinn, buddy, open up, it's your favorite guy in the world!" Mike yelled at the door. Knocking had done nothing to get him inside. Off in the distance, just out of view, the rest of the welcome party waited. Of course, they wouldn't join him on the doorstep. When he still got no answer, he continued to belt out requests to be welcomed inside.

"What the hell do you want?" The door flew open to reveal an angry man with bloodshot eyes and breath that reeked of whiskey. "What is this? Everyone piss off Jinn week? Who's next up to bat?"

"Come on, man, just let me in. This has gone on long enough."

"No." Jinn moved to close the door, but Mike put his hand in the way, stopping him. "You want to lose that hand?"

"Just hear me out, please."

"You know, the last time I heard you out, it ended up with me here. Why the hell would I want to do that again?"

"Look, I'm sorry about that. No one knew it would go that way."

"Well, it did, and I'm done now." A bottle appeared in his hand, and he lifted it to his lips. "So whatever rescue mission you're here to propose, keep it to yourself."

"You don't want to know why I'm here?" Mike pushed. "I've left you alone all this time, because I wanted to respect your boundaries, but it's time that something be done. You can't stay like this, man."

"I'm going to take a wild guess and say that your being here has something to do with the annoying bird of fire that showed up here the other day. She couldn't get to me, so you were called in."

"Perceptive." Mike tapped his head. "You were always one for details."

"Not really. After the hot head flew in, I put up an alarm system and was alerted when you and the rest of your crew arrived."

He peered over the man's shoulder. "You'd think fairies would be better at hiding."

"Great, cat's out of the bag." It was no point in him being on the front line when the entire plan was a bust before they even arrived.

"I'm not helping Nitara, not this time. She made her choice."

"I agree with that. Hell, until I spoke with Inda, I was all for this change you've made. Unfortunately, it's been brought to my attention that it may not have been her choice, not entirely."

"What are you talking about?" Jinn grunted.

"Look, Inda can explain all that. Like I said, your decision about Nitara is yours and I support it. I'm here for something else."

"What could you possibly want from me now?" Jinn sounded like he would put a fist through the wall.

"I know that the reason you're like this isn't entirely because of Nitara." Jinn eased up and allowed the door to open a bit more. Mike was on to something.

"Then what is it about?" Jinn turned from Mike and headed into the house. This was his okay to come in. Mike followed Jinn inside.

"Your wife wasn't the only person you lost that day." The door shut behind him. Apparently, Mike was the only one allowed in; he still had some convincing to do. "Praia is still missing."

"Yes, she is." Jinn took another swig of whiskey before falling onto the couch.

"That's not your fault."

"The hell it isn't!" He slammed the bottle on the table. "If it wasn't for me, she wouldn't have been out there."

"She chose to help, and it wasn't just to save Nitara. If you remember, the entire world was at stake." Mike stood. Jinn wasn't completely placated yet. The man was on the edge and if Mike let his guard down, he might end up out on his ass. "Look, I was going to wait to bring this up, wait until I had something solid, but I think now is a good time to reveal all the cards."

"Spit it out, Mike."

"I think Praia is still alive." Mike said and waited for Jinn to process his announcement.

"Don't play with me, Mike." Jinn pointed at him. "If you're lying, I swear I will hurt you."

"Like I said, I was waiting for a definite response, but yeah, I think she is." Mike swallowed the knot in his throat.

Jinn stepped closer to the man, so close that he thought he might hit him. "What do you know?"

"We searched the entire area where she fell, found everything down there but her. I even got in with some mermaids to help with the search, but there was no trace of our girl. Then we start hearing rumbles about a new djinn hanging out in wolf land. So, I figure we should extend the search that way. I got word about a girl; she can't remember who she is. I think it's her."

"So why haven't you gone to get her?" Jinn nearly growled.

"Well, she is in wolf land, and if this girl is Praia, she is mixed up in some real mess." He stepped back, not wanting to be within arm's reach of the man. "There isn't much that I can do if what we've heard is true. It's gonna take someone much more powerful."

"Fuck." Jinn ran his hand through the dreads that fell around his face.

"Yeah. So, I figured we go and help with Nitara, then perhaps she can use her leverage with the vampires to broker some sort of trade with the wolves."

"That's a long shot." The vampires weren't a generous group. They would want something in return for their help. He was already tired of trading favors. It was the reason he was in this mess to begin with.

"Yeah, it is, but it's a shot. If not, I'm sure we could come up with something." Mike's shoulders relaxed and the breath he'd been holding released.

"Nitara made it pretty damn clear she doesn't want to be with me anymore." Jinn shook his head. He didn't want to go running after her again. Not after what happened the first time around.

"As I mentioned earlier, that isn't exactly her fault." Jinn had been too upset to really consider what Mike or Inda had to say about the woman who crushed his spirit with one blow.

"She told me she is in love with someone else, that I was too late." Maybe it wasn't her fault that she loved someone else. They'd been apart for so long, but it meant that she was no longer his to love. She was no longer his to save.

"Okay, look, what I'm going to say is going to sound far-fetched. Hell, it took me by surprise, and I've seen a lot of crazy shit, but we have proof that it's true."

"Once again, spit it out." Jinn ordered. "You're wasting my time with all this bread crumbing."

"Daegal cursed Nitara. I know you guys were wished free of your bottles or whatever, but he gave her another vessel." He spoke calmly. "Nitara is no longer a free djinn."

"She left me because of a vessel?" It made sense. It also explained why Nitara wasn't affected the same way the others were when she was held captive by Daegal. He didn't need to bind her; she was already his to command. "She could have told me. We could have gotten the vessel and freed her!"

"It wouldn't have been that easy." Mike shook his head.

"No?" Jinn huffed. "You think I can't take any asshole out there?"

"I'm not saying that, man." Mike chuckled. "I know you're a badass, trust me,"

"Then what are you saying?" Jinn balled his fist at his side.

"She left because the vessel ... well, it isn't a normal vessel, Jinn."

"I swear to god, Mike, if you don't just spit this shit out now, I'm going to hurt you." Jinn's jaw tightened as he held back the urge to hit his friend. The man was dangling pertinent information in front of his face.

Mike still hesitated for a moment before finally giving voice to the insanity that was Nitara's current situation. "Her vessel is a vampire."

"What?" Jinn's shoulders dropped. "A vampire is her vessel? How?"

"Look, I won't even pretend to understand what the hell is going on with that, but it's true. Her vessel is the King of the Vampires, and when he called, she had no choice but to go."

"Why didn't she tell me?" Jinn shook his head. "She could have told me. She knows that."

"No idea, but I'm going to suggest that perhaps, he stopped her from doing that." When Jinn didn't have a retort, Mike took that as his cue. "You know, the others are waiting. Sybella is here as well, to help you decide what you want to do here."

"Praia is lost, and Nitara is trapped." Jinn looked out the window where he knew others hid. "When are things gonna get better? Daegal is dead, and he is still fucking up my life."

"Well, think of it this way. We get this all worked out, and then you're done with Daegal and his tampering. Unless the man finds a way back from the dead." Mike laughed.

"You think that's funny, but I wouldn't put it past him." Jinn groaned before waving his hand at the door, which opened. "Tell your minions to come in."

CHAPTER II

Jinn's On Board

"It looks like Inda succeeded."** Graham entered their new hideaway. Shortly after Inda took flight, he found an old rail line that had gone unused for nearly a century. Ardyn worked his magic to make the space more welcoming.

Inside of the tunnel was a fully functioning center of command combined with what some would say was a hotel of five-star amenities. Graham told Ardyn he'd gone overboard, but after the first day, he'd come to see the benefits. Especially the fridge that was always stocked with blood, and it was the good stuff. Besides, it was safer than the rundown old structures that he'd chosen before, especially with Sarah sniffing around.

Every vampire in the region was a suspect. There were very few people he trusted.

"Jinn's on board?" Ardyn perked up in his seat in front of a massive wall of monitors, all of which displayed random images from around the world. Jinn was a key piece to his plans. If the man had decided not to come through, they would have had a hell of a time accomplishing their goal. "That's great news. One less thing to worry about."

"Yes, it took some convincing, but he's coming. Apparently, Nitara crushed him when she left." The vampire grinned, and Ardyn scoffed. Graham was actually happy that Nitara had hurt Jinn. The truth, that they both knew, was that she never would have done it if she didn't feel it was absolutely necessary to protect him.

"I'm sure the knowledge that she didn't have a choice in the matter helps relieve his worries." For Ardyn's offered opinion, he received a glaring frown.

"Actually, no. They had to sell him on it with the promise of saving some girl from wolf territory." Graham cracked open a bottle of blood from the stocked fridge. "It would appear that getting his wife back isn't as big of a prize as it was the first time around."

"I can imagine it wouldn't be." He went back to tinkering on his latest project until Graham's delivered message completely registered with him. "Wait, what did you say? Why would they need to go to wolf territory?"

"No idea. I didn't ask too many more questions. Once wolves were mentioned, I lost interest, no offense."

"Yeah, none taken." He frowned. Graham should have asked more questions. He should have gotten every detail available.

"Are you worried they may ask you to tag along?" Graham teased. He knew how much Ardyn wanted to avoid his home. Yeah, he would have loved to be welcomed back with open arms, but that wasn't going to happen. Ardyn was changed, and wolves—hell, all the shifters—as ironic as it sounded, were against change.

"No, not at all." Even if they begged the man to go, he wouldn't. His concern was Nitara. Once she was free, he was done with rescue missions.

"Good, so we can move on." If Ardyn wasn't signing up for the second leg of the party, there would be no sense in discussing it further. "What's the latest? Any word from Nitara?"

"As a matter of fact, no. I haven't heard from her since our last run-in when you nearly ruined everything." He rolled his eyes. "I've been trying not to reach out to her. Figured it would be best if she lie low right now. Didn't want to call any unnecessary attention to her."

"Look, I already explained myself for that. When are you going to let it go?"

"Yeah, you did. And no, I won't. I'll keep busting your balls about it regardless of explanation." It was the same thing Graham would have done to him if he'd taken such a foolish risk. Hell, Graham still busted his balls for the one time he'd been seen running through the fields too close to the general population. A human girl witnessed his blaze of blue fur cutting through the woods. If Graham hadn't caught her before she got to the others, the entire world would have known about Ardyn. That was something they wanted to avoid for as long as possible. Especially when he was so unsure of himself and had very little control over his powers. It would have been a recipe for disaster.

"We need to find a way to get to her and figure out what the hell is going on." Graham needed to refocus the conversation. Ardyn could toss all the jabs he wanted later.

"I have eyes on the inside. I'll check it out."

"Eyes? What eyes?" Graham stalked over to him. "You didn't tell me about any surveillance on the inside."

"As if I would tell you, the man who has problems keeping his mouth shut!"

"Oh, ha, ha." Graham thought about keeping the next bit of information to himself, but figured he would share it with the hybrid. "Sarah came to see me."

"Sarah? As in wife of our enemy?" Ardyn dropped what he was doing. "Now this is information that needs to be shared! Spill."

"She wanted to buddy up to me. Tried to get me to agree to work with her." Graham finished off the bottle of blood and dropped the empty container into the trash.

"Did she throw herself at you?" Grinning, Ardyn waggled his eyebrows. Graham had some juicy gossip, and Ardyn wanted every drop.

"Yeah, as if that was appealing." Graham laughed. "You should have seen her; she basically shook her ass in my face."

"Are you telling me that you weren't even the tiniest bit tempted to take her offer?" It had been so long since Ardyn had a female shake anything in his direction. He got aroused just thinking of the prospect.

"The woman isn't loyal to the husband she has. Why would I trust her to be loyal to me?" Graham had had enough of tawdry flings. If he was going to be with someone, it had to mean more. Mindless sex no longer pleased him, and that was all Sarah could ever offer him.

"Question is, why would she even think of coming to you?" Ardyn narrowed his gaze. As far as he knew it, Graham was enemy number one for the current royal family. Sarah had to have a reason to think that she could approach him in such a way. "Did something happen between the two of you?"

"Perhaps." Graham shrugged and winked at the inquiring man.

"Oh, now you get tight lipped?" Ardyn crossed his arms over his chest and stared at Graham. "Now is not the time to be hiding things, man. I need to know everything, especially if it affects how people are going to respond to what we have going on here."

"Dammit." Graham groaned because he knew Ardyn was right. His partner needed to know everything, but Graham wanted to keep his secrets. That was how he'd survived, nothing that didn't need to be told ever was. "She was the one who told me about Nitara's bond to Tyrellis."

"What?" Ardyn couldn't believe what he was hearing. He'd been tiptoeing around the secret, trying not to spill the beans and here it was. Sarah had been dishing it out freely.

"Yeah. Cass was making his move, and she somehow knew that I cared about Nitara. So she came to me with the information, knowing that I would do whatever it took to stop Cass in order to save Nitara. She couldn't make the move on her own. It would raise too much suspicion."

"Well, isn't she the resourceful one?" Ardyn chuckled.

"Now that the cat is out of the bag, and she's worried about her position." Graham explained.

"Understandably." Ardyn thought about the information received. "Oh shit. You and Nitara have been seen out together, haven't you? At that bar?"

"Yeah, so what?" Graham nodded.

"Well, now that you know their dirty little secret, she may take that as a threat. What if she tells Tyrellis?"

"She wouldn't tell him she betrayed him. The man is a nutcase." Considering the idea, Graham wondered if Sarah might find a way around telling Tyrellis what she did. It wouldn't be unlike her. "You think we need to do something about her?"

"No, I think it is a problem that will work itself out. I doubt you were her last stop on the 'holy fuck, save me' train ride." Ardyn pulled out a small screen from a compartment in his station. "Right now, our focus needs to be on Nitara."

"What are you doing?" Graham peered over his shoulder.

"This little baby allows me to see inside places deemed unfit for my kind. It keeps a few days of history on file. It's like a surveillance system without having to get inside to wire up a bunch of cameras. The bugs travel inside on visitors and just hang out. Right now, I'm searching for the last sighting of Nitara."

"Wait there, go back." Graham tapped the screen. Ardyn rewound the image. "She went into his room? Can we see inside?"

"Yep, just switch views, and there." The two looked at Nitara and Tyrellis inside his room. Even on the screen, the tension between the two was palpable.

"He doesn't look pleased, does he?"

"No, he doesn't."

"Is there any sound?" Graham frowned. "We need to be able to hear what's going on."

"Only on the live feed. I haven't been able to work out the playback issue."

They watched as the two spoke. The tension increased, and then Tyrellis pulled out the photograph. Their fears about Sarah came true; why else would he have that image? Why else would he be upset about it suddenly after years of the two speaking with each other? Moments later, a worked up Tyrellis forced Nitara to return to the space inside of him and walked out of the room.

"That can't be good." Graham stepped away. "How long ago was that?"

"Looks like a few days." Ardyn frowned. "You know, she told me about how it works, how he pulls her into him, but I would have never imagined that. It's so messed up!"

"No one's seen her since?" Graham wanted to think of anything but the disturbing scene they'd just witnessed.

"Not that I'm picking up. This is really going to make things more difficult for us." Ardyn put the screen down.

"We have to figure out a way to work around this."

"Should be simple enough, getting a djinn out of a vampire. Yeah, no problem." Ardyn hadn't planned on needing to extract Nitara from Tyrellis. He had no idea how they were going to make that happen.

Nitara could fashion her unwanted vessel to resemble something other than the hollow chest cavity of a walking dead man. Despite her efforts to disguise things, she couldn't get past the stale scent of decay or the echoes of his lunacy that played like eerie background noise to every moment of her time spent trapped inside of him. She had to get out. By her calculations, it had already been a few days, longer than she'd been inside in quite a while. The only time he'd kept her tucked away that long was when Daegal first created their bond. He didn't trust that she couldn't break it and refused to let her out.

She'd started her normal routine of bugging the master to irritate him into releasing her, but it wasn't working out in her favor. The first couple of days went as planned. Tyrellis begged and pleaded for her to stop, but she was relentless. She tortured him with rock music that induced headaches and the sounds of whale calls. That was one that she lucked out on after overhearing him talk about how much the sound annoyed him. She did a lot more than just irritate him with noise. She made him recall horrible things that he'd done to people, and the things that he'd made her do. It was an ever-running list that played on a loop. Usually, after the first few hours of mental recaps, Tyrellis gave up and sent her on her way. This wasn't the usual occasion.

It wasn't long before her efforts to drive him mad backfired. His increasing insanity seemed to cross over to her. Though she eased back, the damage had already been done. The ramblings of his mind bled through the wall of her false surroundings and flooded her own nerve endings. Soon her head filled with thoughts of death and regrets that were not her own. Each time she thought it was over, that he had found some semblance of peace, Nitara would double over. Her hands clutched the side of her head as the wailing began once again.

"Why are you here?" Cass looked over his glass at the vampire he'd only seen up close one time before as he was being kicked out of her home. It was right after her husband had taken over. When Cass made it clear that he wouldn't be one of the ones to kiss up to the new ruler, they gave him the boot from the chosen land.

"I come to you with an offer." Sarah frowned at the surroundings. This wasn't Cast's usual spot, but he'd been lying low since his run-in with Nitara. "Why else would I come to this dump?"

"An offer? What could you possibly have to offer me?" Sarah wasn't a fan of Cass and that was no secret. She made sure that he and his followers suffered for their refusal to fall in line. Tyrellis wasn't the monster he was painted to be. Everyone knew it was Sarah whispering her seeds of evil into his ear.

"Reverie, of course." She remained standing in front of him as the smile spread across her face. "That is what you want, isn't it? I'm here to offer it to you, if you agree to my terms."

Cast sat up in his seat. "Excuse me?" There had to be a catch. Why would she be there to give him anything? He scouted the bar, checking for her minions, but she had come without her usual entourage. In fact, they were completely alone. Even the bartender had disappeared.

"Yes, Cast. You want it, and I'm offering it to you." She looked at the empty seat at his table, requesting permission she didn't need to join him. He slid it out with his foot, and with a frown, she sat on the chair that looked as if it hadn't been cleaned in a decade.

"Why would you want to offer Reverie to me? Why would you turn your back on Tyrellis now?" Sarah made a good show of being the loyal wife. Yes, she was conniving, evil to her core. No one doubted that, but she was devoted to Tyrellis. Or at least she was good at making everyone believe she was.

"All things must come to an end. Even the immortals have an expiration date. I fear there is an end in sight for my husband." She waved to the bartender, who had been peeking through a side door. He quickly brought her a drink. Everyone knew her favorite and kept on hand for her. After he gave her the drink, he hustled out of the front door.

"Are you telling me that you've decided to jump ship before it happens?" He laughed. It was classic, yet unexpected. The king was going down and those closest to him were holding knives behind their backs. Who would have thought the queen would be the first to draw her blade to stab him?

"I'm being proactive." She sipped from her drink, unfazed by the man's obvious judgements. "Look, either you accept my offer of help, or you don't. It is obvious you will make a move for the throne as soon as it is open. Right now, you have a choice; decide if you want to succeed, because I can promise you that without my help, you will fail."

"If Tyrellis is going down, why shouldn't I just wait to make my move? When the little genie bitch isn't a problem, I'll have no issue with taking what's mine." Cass had already spun a web in his mind that ended with him in the very place he wanted to be. He would rule Reverie and his people would no longer suffer under the hands of the prick whose wife didn't even believe in his ability to rule.

"That just shows how simple-minded you really are." She leaned across the table. "Waiting won't work for you because Graham is the one that's going to take him down. Do you think you can stand against him and win?" She knew he couldn't. The two had already faced each other, and it didn't end well for the younger contender.

"How do you know that?" His jaw squared as he pushed the glass around on the table.

"Don't worry about how I know what I know." Polishing off her drink, Sarah stood from her seat. She circled the table with slow, deliberate steps that pushed her hips out and gave her body a curvy appearance that wasn't entirely natural to her form. As she reached his side of the table, she dragged a well-manicured nail up his arm and rested her palms on his shoulder. Confident hands massaged his shoulders. "What I suggest is that we strike before Graham does. Claim your right before Graham can make his move and he will have no choice but to secede."

"What do you have planned?" Cass rolled his neck, enjoying her touch. "You wouldn't be here if you didn't have a solid plan in mind. What is it?"

"Not here." She leaned in close to his ear, and as she slipped a piece of paper into his pocket, she whispered, "Meet me in two hours."

CHAPTER 12

The Gathering

"**I**nda, come out! I know you're in there!" Jax realized where Inda was when it became clear that Briar and all the key members of her guard had left Vilar. The dragon was quick to take flight despite the fairies who tried to keep him at bay. He landed on Jinn's lawn and called for the woman until she was forced by the others to face him.

"What the hell do you want?" Inda, the woman who still owned his heart, finally came out after Jinn threatened to put both her and her hot-headed ex into a bottle together if they didn't work out their differences. If anyone could do it, it was him.

"What do I want?" He paced the ground. "You come back here now … no wait, you've been here for years, but you chose not to tell me. How can you stand there and ask me what I want? I want an explanation, Inda."

"Too bad. I don't owe you one." She turned, ready to storm back into the house, but the door she'd left open slammed in her face. "Fuck," she cursed at the djinn under her breath. Of course, Jinn would force her to deal with her ex. Hell, it was what she was doing to him.

"You don't? You left me high and dry, and then you return without a word. The entire damn world knows you're here, except me! I'm supposed to be the love of your life."

"Love of my life?" Inda laughed. "You think a lot of yourself!"

"I'm sorry. Are you telling me that those weren't your exact words?" Jax kept his distance and stood on the curb. He knew the woman—if he came an inch closer before she was ready, she'd explode. She stood on the porch staring down at him with hands on her hips and an expression on her face that warned him to stay away.

"Yeah, I said that, but that was before you kicked me to the curb for being loyal to my people." She paced the small area on the porch. "You were my everything until you demanded that I give up everything for you!"

"I made no such demands."

"Liar!" her scream echoed in the empty streets and scared a family of birds from their home in a nearby tree. "You wanted everything from me, even when it meant that you would have to give up nothing! I couldn't believe you could be so damn selfish."

"I wanted you here with me." He stared at her. "I didn't think that was such a bad thing."

"I told you I would be back!" Her hands flailed, punctuating her frustration with the conversation and the man in front of her.

"Yes, you did, but when? For all we knew, you would have to be gone for centuries. You were so willing to give up all that time together."

"If you loved me as much as you claimed to, the time wouldn't have mattered!"

"Really? You expected me to wait centuries when it would only seem like a few years to you at best? And you call me the selfish one?" Finally, he approached her. He was fed up with being treated like the villain in their relationship.

"Yes, Jax, you are selfish because you think the world revolves around you. Well, it doesn't!"

"Give me a break, Indy!" He stepped closer again, but she stepped back, retaining the distance between them.

"Don't call me that." She shook her head. "You don't have the right to call me that!"

"Now I can't call you by your name? Do you hate me that much?" His hands fell to his side. "Why do I deserve this from you?"

"That's not my name. And no, I don't hate you. To hate you would mean I'd have to give a damn about you."

"If you care so little, why have you been hiding from me?" He challenged her, and she flinched. He saw it then in her eyes. She cared even if she wanted him and the rest of the world to believe that she didn't.

"Hiding? I haven't been hiding from you." Inda stomped away from the house and the prying eyes and ears of those inside. "If your ego was any bigger, there wouldn't be room for the rest of us on this planet!"

"Ego? Right, so it's because of my ego that you swore Briar to secrecy?" He followed her on her path down the abandoned suburban street.

"I don't have to explain anything to you." She stopped walking. "Stop following me, Jax!" Unleashing her wings, she took to the sky. He, of course, followed her path. Until they landed in the middle of what had once been a thriving cattle farm, but now was the home to overgrown fields of sunburnt grass.

"Inda, I'm not here to fight you." Jax's feet planted on the ground as his dragon retreated.

"Well, you're doing a hell of a good job with that." She groaned. "Why can't you just leave me alone?"

"I came to talk to you," Jax huffed. "Why is that so hard for you to do? Why do you have such a problem with talking to me?"

"So, talk. What do you want?"

"I want you back. I miss you. Even after these years, it's you I want. Ever since I heard you were back; my mind is consumed with thoughts of you. And here you are, just as hotheaded and annoying as ever, yet I still want nothing more than to pull you into my arms." He was the one pacing now as Inda watched. "I was so angry at you for years after you left. I thought about what I would do or say if I ever saw you again. This is not it. This is not the fight I thought we would have. Instead of burning the sky with my rage, I just wish that you were mine again, that I could take it all back and do it right. Knowing that you have been back here all this time and avoiding me, I know I fucked up."

"Jax." Inda wasn't expecting his confession. She expected hours of fighting followed by the two of them going their separate ways, but that wasn't the case. She was caught completely off guard. "I can't deal with this. Not right now, not with everything going on."

"Fine, I understand that. Handle your business, but I'm not going anywhere."

"You're just going to hang around?" She sucked her teeth. "Why?"

"What else does the prince of dragons have to do?" He shrugged. "My brothers can handle official business."

"This won't end the way you want it to." Inda pointed at him. "You're wasting your time."

"I'm almost positive about that." He shrugged. "But I've already waited this long. What's a few more days?"

When they returned to the home turned HQ, the door was standing open, no longer locking her outside with her estranged ex. The crew on the inside felt that she'd successfully faced her issues. Jax had followed her back to the house; apparently, he meant that he literally wasn't going to go anywhere until they'd handle their issues. She wanted nothing to do with it. Already she was trying to calculate a way to escape him, but she would have to wait.

"What are you doing?" Inda looked over her shoulder to her unwanted follower.

"I'm coming inside," he responded, as if it should have been obvious.

"Why?"

"I was asked to help." Jax smiled.

"Excuse me?" She rolled her eyes. "Who the hell asked you for help?"

"Jinn and I are friends. He called me to ask for my assistance with your problem with Reverie."

"You've got to be fucking kidding me." She scoffed as she stomped forward. Why the hell did they need help from the dragon? Jinn was trying to mess with her head. She was sure of it.

"He's not kidding. And if you don't mind coming inside, we can get this show on the road." Jinn stood in the now open door with a look of exasperation. "I think we've wasted enough time as it is."

Inda stomped into the house with Jax on her tail. She muttered about betrayal and bullshit, but neither Jinn nor Jax attempted to decipher the flurry of curses.

"Are you two done?" Mike couldn't help the question that fell from his mouth.

"Fuck off." Inda flipped him the bird as she stomped past him and to the kitchen. "I need a drink!"

We need to get in there. Nitara is missing and now Tyrellis is in hiding. What the fuck is going on in there?" Graham barked at Ardyn—who worked to repair the lost connection—while he paced the floor.

"I'm working on it. I don't know what happened. None of my surveillance bugs are functioning." He furiously tapped on the console.

"Which means someone found us out!" Graham couldn't contain his anger, no matter how much he tried. "If someone figured out they were being watched, how long do you think it would be until they trace it back to us?"

"That's impossible." Ardyn lifted his eyes to the vampire. "How would they have known? They are literally bugs."

"You really think so?" Graham stopped in front of Ardyn, who wiped sweat from his brow and cracked open another beer.

"So, tell me, why aren't they working? Look, we already know that Sarah was plotting against Tyrellis, and therefore, against us. Who knows how many people she has on her side?"

"You think Sarah was strong enough to kill my bugs?" Ardyn refused to believe that any vampire could do that. He'd been using them for years and not a single one had ever been disabled.

"No, but I think she is cunning enough to know that they were there and to find someone to destroy them for her." Sarah was resourceful; they all knew that. If she wanted something done, she would find a way.

"Fuck." Ardyn hadn't considered that Sarah would have gotten outside magical help. "Who the hell would help her?"

"You know as well as I do that there are beings who have defected from just about every group. It wouldn't be that hard for her to find a wayward witch, especially after everything that happened with that badass warlock. They're all scrambling to make new alliances. Sarah is just smart enough to use that to her advantage."

"You're right, we need to get in there. But we can't move yet, not until Inda gets back here with the others." Ardyn gave up on his bugs and conjured a beer.

"Well, I suggest we light a fire under their asses. We're running out of time." Graham left the new hideout in search of a beverage that was a lot more intoxicating.

"We need to get moving." Inda returned from the kitchen with a drink in her hand. "Just got a call from Reverie and it seems things are moving pretty quickly. Nitara is missing and Ardyn thinks that Tyrellis' wife is up to no good."

"Damn! Well, how long do we have?" Mike considered his wife and new daughter. He would have to call her and explain what was happening.

"He wants us there like yesterday," Inda spoke, avoiding any form of interaction with Jax.

"Let's get things in order. Sybella, thank you for your help here." Briar nodded to Mysti, who was preparing to return the seer back to the safety of Vilar.

"I haven't done anything." She shrugged. She still hadn't spent any time with Jinn and was already being ushered off back to her home.

"Actually, perhaps you can be of some use. Nitara is missing. Last time, you were able to give Jinn a mental connection to her, to let us know where she was. Do you think you can do that again?" Mike offered.

"Yes, if he is willing." She peered over at the djinn. He'd been conveniently quiet during the conversation. All eyes turned to Jinn; silence punctuated the lingering pause as they waited to see what he would say.

"Sure, why the hell not? If it will help to get this shit over with and get you all out of my living room, let's just do it." Jinn shrugged, and the others sighed in unison.

Nitara curled in on herself. She rocked beneath the pressure of Tyrellis's insanity. It was growing more and more each day. The weight of his paranoia was only made more so with the growing suspicions of his wife, who reportedly spent more and more time away from home and in the areas known for his rivals. He screamed internally about his fear and the pain of her betrayal. For Nitara, it was overwhelming.

There were times, when he was particularly fragile, when she could witness, from within, the outside world. The shade that existed over her would fade away and she could see what things looked like around him. She watched as he finally confronted Sarah.

"Tell me the truth!" he demanded with a trembling voice.

"What truth is it you want from me?" Sarah rolled her eyes as if the conversation was a waste of her time. "You have truly lost your mind, Tyrellis."

"Have I? Or is the truth that you are conspiring against me? All this time you've been trying to convince me that the world is at my back, knife in hand, and yet it's you I should have been concerned about. Isn't it?"

"Are you serious?" She frowned. "You accuse me of betraying you? What have I done but stand by your side all these years, and now you doubt me?"

"I can feel it, the blade in my back!" he hissed at her. "You are not with me the way you were before. Admit it!"

"I will not stand here and be disrespected like this." Sarah turned, ready to storm out of the room, but Tyrellis grabbed her by the arm and turned her back to face him.

"You will stand here and take whatever I give you! I am the king!" Tyrellis yelled as his fingers dug into her skin; blood dripped from her arm where sharp nails pierced her flesh.

"King? What kind of king are you? You're holed up in this room, rambling about betrayals and letting your paranoia consume you! Who do you rule?" She sneered as she pulled her arm from his hold. "Do you think these people who merely tolerate you will stand beside you? Do you think they will lift your sad ass up from the hole you've dug? You had every opportunity to step up and be an outstanding leader. Instead, you coward behind your genie and use her power to keep them in line. You are no king! You're a scared little boy and everyone knows it!"

The sound of Tyrellis's hand against Sarah's cheek echoed in the large room. She didn't cry. In fact, she didn't make a sound. With her cheek red where his palm contacted with her flesh, she faced him with anger in her eyes. "Is that the best you can do? Like I said, you're nothing but a little boy."

Nitara felt it, finally. Tyrellis was going to let her free. She stood from the ball she was curled into and prepared for her release. As he called to her internally, she rejoiced. Finally! Nitara couldn't celebrate because just as the door opened, it slammed shut again. She reached out toward the light that would usually free her, but pulled back with a howling scream as it burned her.

Tyrellis' scream echoed Nitara's as she pulled her hand into her. Still viewing his world, she saw the straps that bound him. Crossing his chest, they burned through his clothing and melted into his flesh. Quickly, he healed. His skin melded with the binding and sealed them within his body.

"What the hell is this?" He pulled at the straps, but they wouldn't move.

"This is my contingency plan. I knew you would turn on me. It was only a matter of time before that paranoia of yours switched to focus on me." The doors opened and Cass strolled into the room with a sickly grin on his face.

"Honey, I'm home!" The man clapped his hands and laughed.

"How could you do this to me?" Tyrellis still clawed at the straps around his body.

"Change is inevitable, my dear." Sarah touched his face, then dragged her nails across his jaw and licked her lips as his face bled. "You know how much I like to be prepared."

"You will pay for this." Tyrellis groaned.

"Really? Tell me, how do you see that happening now that you can't call upon your little puppet to fix things for you?" Sarah pushed the man to the floor. "You are nothing without her! Just a sad, weak little man with no strength of his own!"

Tyrellis froze on the floor where he landed. She was right about him. It was the fear that drove his paranoia. Without Nitara, he was powerless against the older vampires.

"Take him away. I'm sick of looking at his pathetic face!" Sarah yelled, and Cass instructed two of his men to carry the frozen king away.

As they hauled his body away, Nitara could see less and less of the outside world. The final snickers of the woman who betrayed Tyrellis were the last she heard before everything went dark, and then there was a silence so deafening that it hurt her head. She turned to return to her corner, but before she could curl in on herself again, a familiar voice replaced the rambling sounds of her vessel's mind.

"Nitara, can you hear me?" The deep timbre of his voice soothed her. This was not the first time he'd entered her mind.

"Jinn?" Nitara felt warmth return to her heart, but it wasn't there for long.

"Are you okay?" He sounded indifferent. His concern for her wasn't that of a lover. It wasn't that of a husband in search of the wife who'd been taken away. She'd broken him, his heart, his spirit.

"Yes," she lied.

"Your friends are trying to find you; I need to know where you are." There it was. Her friends were trying to find her, not him. He didn't want to find her.

"Trapped inside of my vessel," she stated plainly.

"The vampire."

"You know about him?"

"Yes. Are you not able to get out?" He paused. "Will he not let you?"

"You know how this works; he has to allow me to leave. Unfortunately, he couldn't give me permission now, even if he wanted to." She looked down at her hand where the flesh still stung.

"What do you mean?"

"Sarah, his wife, she betrayed him. She's working with Cass, the leader of the rebels who stands against Tyrellis. I'm not sure what magic she used, but she bound Tyrellis so that he cannot release me."

"Fuck." Jinn's voice was full of disappointment and frustration.

"Yeah, it's another shitty situation." Nitara's shoulders dropped in defeat.

"Where are you now?" Jinn asked. "Did they take your vessel somewhere?"

"I don't know. They moved him, but he shut me out. I doubt we're outside of his compound. That would be too risky right now. Sarah is going to want to keep Tyrellis close by."

"Okay, good. Help is coming." Help was coming, he wasn't. She had to reconcile that for herself.

"Jinn, thank you." She appreciated his help, even though she didn't deserve it. She needed him to know that.

"Yeah." Again, indignation coated his voice, and then it was silent again. He was gone, and she was alone.

"Well?" Briar leaned into Jinn, barely giving him room to breathe after coming out of Sybella's hold.

"It's not good." Jinn stood, to give himself space from the overbearing woman. "She is trapped."

"Trapped?" the fairy queen asked as she handed him a glass of ice water.

"Yeah. Apparently, Sarah, his wife, stabbed him in the back. She is working with someone powerful enough to fashion a device to hold the vampire. Whatever it is, it has locked Nitara inside of him." He swallowed the water in two gulps and wiped the sweat from his brow. "Oh, and there is some vampire boy toy named Cass that is helping the vamp queen."

"Cass," Jax groaned, remembering the ice dragon with the similar name who they had to put down for helping Daegal. "What do they do, breed them at a damn factory?"

"Shit," Mike groaned. "It's never easy, is it? Who the hell could have that kind of power?"

"Yeah." Jinn looked at Inda. "You better update Ardyn. Let him know were headed that way." He stood from the seat holding the glass in his hand, and as he exited the room, it filled with whiskey.

"All right, let's get to it!" Mike clapped and everyone groaned.

CHAPTER 13

Sarah's Plan

"**W**hat happens now?" **Cass stood** in front of Sarah with his arms spread out at his sides. He was being carefully fitted for his new attire. Already he was happy with the good life. The women who measured him made flirty glances and giggled whenever he shot them a wink. Yeah, being king was going to be good.

As it was, he did everything that Sarah told him to do. Didn't see the point in stirring up any trouble. The woman was on top because she knew what she was doing. He told himself he would learn all he could from her, and then kick her to the curb just like she did Tyrellis. Perhaps he would be a bit kinder. He shuddered to think what the woman was putting the former leader through, but reports were that he was being tortured by something terrible. That wasn't his concern. His focus was on making sure she stayed happy with him. Sarah felt he needed new threads if he was going to be their next leader. When presented to the public, he couldn't look, as she put it, unkempt.

"Is it necessary for me to dress like this?" He asked, his displeasure clear in his tone.

"What exactly is your problem with the attire?" Sarah was disappointed in his aversion to stylish wear.

"This isn't me." He peered over the head of the woman who measured his chest to the reflection of him in the half-made suit. "I look ridiculous."

"You look like you fit the part. Did you really think you could rule while wearing tattered jeans and leather jackets? You have to look like a ruler if you expect anyone to show you any kind of respect." She waved her hand and rejected the brightly colored fabric the short woman who assisted the designer showed her. "When you're in power, you will have to hobnob with all the who's who of the supernatural world. They'll expect you to be on your best behavior, and to look like a decent person."

"What are you talking about?" After stepping down from the pedestal, he picked up a glass of spiked wine. He sipped from it, and his eyes widened with pleasure as the mixture awakened his taste buds and aroused his lower half. "Man, I can definitely get used to this. Booze doesn't taste anywhere near this good at the bar! What's this talk about the who's who? Vampires don't mix with the others."

"The common vampire, no, but the leader, yes." Sarah would have to teach Cass literally everything about being in charge of Reverie. "You need to educate yourself, strive to be better than the leader before you. There are a lot of things that go with ruling, Cassius, and that is something you'll have to learn."

"Cass, the name is Cass.," he corrected her before he polished off his drink.

"No. Your name is Cassius, and that is the name you'll go by from now on." She grabbed his hand before he could pick up another glass. If he was going to absorb anything, it would be the lessons she had to teach, not the endless flow of wine.

"I'm not about this, changing who I am to fit who you think I should be. Hate to break it to you babe, but I'm me, Cast, leader of the outlaws and now King of Reverie! I do what I want." He pulled away from her and sat on the plush couch, where he had a nice view of the ample ass of the seamstress. "You want to change my image, my name, and what else?"

"If you want a list, I have one." She winked at him playfully.

"We need to talk about how things are going to go here." Cassius had only been king for a day and already the power was going to his head.

"Yes, we do." Sarah turned to Rebecca, the designer who had been quietly working at her task right along with the seamstress, who was enjoying her flirtatious tease with Cassius. "Give us some time, please." The designer and her pouty assistant left.

"What's the story here?" When they were alone, Cassius got up and grabbed that second glass.

"What?" She eyed his hand. "Now is not the time for you to get drunk."

"I'm fine." He waved off her concern. "Tyrellis isn't completely out of the picture until he is dead. When do we make that happen?"

"We can't just kill him. We have to do this the right way." Sarah slipped from a mothering tone to a sultry one. With the drink in his hand and the bulge in his pants, she could see that a softer touch would work much better. "Right now, he is driving himself mad, especially with having Nitara trapped inside of him."

"And that's good for us?" He watched her hips as she walked across the room and pushed the door shut to give them more privacy.

"Yes, the people will see how unstable he is. Then you can appear and challenge him. It will be a fight that you will win, obviously, and as rules state, if you challenge the leader and win, you take his place."

"You say it as if it is so simple." The light that bounced off the pale skin of her cleavage worked in a hypnotic way. Cassius found himself entranced by her.

"Well, no, it isn't that simple. We have to make sure we give him enough time." Sarah was back at his side and pulling the jacket off his shoulders. Running her hand across his bare chest, she purred.

"Enough time for what?" Cassius swallowed his arousal and tried to stay focused, but her touch was exhilarating, and his lower mind was completely preoccupied with thoughts of her.

"Enough time to make sure that whatever he says, it sounds so outlandish that no one will be willing to believe him. As it is, he has been missing for a while. It's starting to inspire a lot of speculation. The next summit is just a few days away. The city mayors will all be here in the capital. That is when we will strike. By then, he should be good and ripe."

"Wait, what makes you think one of the mayors won't want to take over? What if they jump in line ahead of me?"

"They won't." She rolled her eyes. "Do you know anything about the structure of things? If not, I suggest you read up. No mayor can challenge the king during an official summit. If they want to, they have to wait until Tyrellis calls things to a close. You will challenge him before that. As a citizen, it is your right."

"This is all moving really fast." Cassius hadn't considered that he would need to challenge Tyrellis officially, or that he would have to do it with all the eyes of the vampire world on him. The summit was televised to all vampire sectors.

"Cold feet?" She nuzzled him before replacing the jacket with one that was finished.

"No, just a head rush." He turned to his reflection in the mirror and adjusted the collar. "You know, I look pretty damn good."

"See," she kissed his neck, "you fit the role." Sarah walked in front of Cast, blocking his view of himself but giving him the sight of her backside reflected in the mirror. Her lips danced across his chest and her hand roamed his body in a southern trajectory.

"You're still a married woman." He looked down to find her wide eyes staring up at him as her tongue teased his nipple.

"Are you telling me that you care?" she purred, shocked at his sudden concern for what was decent and fair.

"No, not one damn bit." Cassius turned and scooped the woman into his arms. He carried her to the bed at the back of the room. "Yeah, being king is definitely going to be fun!" He growled as he carelessly ripped through lacey fabric.

"There are some interesting rumors going on out there," Graham stated when he returned to the hideout from a run. He'd decided to try to go out and get more information since the bugs were disabled. Their recon would have to take a more traditional form. Things around Tyrellis' compound had gone quiet, too quiet for comfort, and he wasn't down for sitting and speculating about what was happening.

"Oh, yeah?" Ardyn stood from the fridge, where he searched for the second half of a sandwich he'd been waiting to eat. "What type of rumors?"

160

"Tyrellis is down for the count and people are saying Cassius is the one who did it." Sitting down at the counter, Graham watched him.

"That makes no sense." Ardyn spoke with his head in the fridge.

"It does if Sarah got to him," Graham huffed. "What the hell are you doing? I'm trying to relay important information to you here!"

"I'm looking for my damn sandwich. This is crazy. I know I put it in here." He continued shifting things around, the same ten things he'd shifted about twenty times and still hadn't found what he was looking for.

"Your what?" Graham leaned forward. "While you're in there, hand me a drink."

"It was an Italian beef, man. It took forever to conjure that damn thing, and it tastes just like the ones we used to get in Chicago. And it's gone." Ardyn tossed a drink to the vampire and went from the fridge to the freezer, hoping his search there would turn up with better results.

"You mean that greasy thing that was in there?" Graham sipped from the bottle and paused as he caught the angry gleam in Ardyn's eyes.

"Greasy thing?" Ardyn stood. "What did you do?"

"I thought it was spoiled. I threw it out."

"You did what?" he slammed the door to the fridge so hard that it bounced back and hit him in the shoulder.

"Sorry, I didn't think it would be a big thing." When Ardyn growled, Graham realized he needed to diffuse the situation. "Man, you need a nap or something?"

"A nap?" Ardyn growled and his skin took on a green hue. His eyes glowed, and he clutched the handle hard enough to bend the metal.

"Okay, wrong thing to say." He stood. "Just make another one."

"It took hours to create the first one." Ardyn had to pull the sandwich from his memory. He had to think of the flavors that teased his tongue whenever he had one. It had been years since he'd had one made by the old man in his pack. A recipe passed down through one family, one that he missed like hell.

"Hours?" Cocking his head to the side, he looked at the man, and cautiously accessed his condition. "What's going on that it took you hours to create a sandwich?"

"I'm exhausted, and that flavor is very specific!" Ardyn slammed his fist on the counter. "Fuck, I wanted that!"

"Okay, so take a nap," Graham suggested again. "You clearly need rest."

"Whatever." Defeated, Ardyn waved his hand and a slab of ribs appeared. Graham watched in awe as he inhaled the full slab, then waved his hand and another replaced the one he'd just devoured.

"See. Feel better?"

"It's not the same," Ardyn grunted. "But yeah, better."

"Do you think you can focus enough for me to tell you about what I found out?"

"Yeah, spill." Ardyn wiped the sauce from his face.

"Cast is with Sarah. That's not exactly what everyone is saying, but I know it." Relaxing, he returned to his seat across from the man who appeared to be sane again. "It makes sense. She approached me, I refused, and she went to the next option."

"Cast is the next option? Is there no one better?"

"No one dumb enough to do what she wants him to do. Besides, something is telling me that she isn't planning on keeping him employed for long." Graham gave him a knowing look.

"A play for power." Ardyn finished off the second plate and a beer replaced the plate. "Doesn't look like she is taking her time about it, either. Good thing we have help coming."

"Shit, when are they supposed to be here?" Graham had forgotten about the cavalry that was supposed to be coming from the south, led in by his hot-headed friend.

"Aw, it sounds like my buddy missed me." Inda appeared at the entrance. She looked around the space, which had changed a lot since she left. "Hey, I like what you've done with the place. It's a lot more hotel than hostel now."

"Well, it's about damn time you got back here." Graham ignored the compliment given to Ardyn. "Where's everyone else? I thought you said you were able to convince them to come."

"I did. And thank you for making me feel so damn welcomed!" She rolled her eyes. "I fly halfway across the world to help you and I don't even get so much as a thank you."

"Inda, I apologize for his manners." Ardyn shot Graham a look; the man was always causing problems. "I hope your trip back wasn't too difficult. Thank you for taking the risk of that journey for us. Are your companions far behind?"

"See, that wasn't so hard to do!" She stuck her tongue out at Graham and gave Ardyn a hug to exaggerate the moment. "Yes, Ardyn, they're right behind me. Shouldn't be long until they arrive. We didn't want to all come in at once, might look too suspicious if anyone is paying attention."

"I'm sure Sarah has quite a few eyes out there." Graham wasn't fazed by her display. He was still focused on the business at hand. "She suspects that I'll be making a move on Tyrellis. Even if she isn't searching for you, her bugs will be watching out for anything out of the ordinary."

"With the party we have coming, there will be plenty of that." Inda took a seat at the table covered in maps and jottings from Ardyn's theories on how to get inside of Tyrellis' home. "But don't worry, we were careful."

"What's the crew looking like?" Ardyn joined her at the table and gathered his things. Most of the stuff seemed incoherent to even him. He didn't need anyone to see it and think he was crazy.

"You know, a few djinn, a dragon or two, a sprinkle of fairies … the standard rescue party." Inda shrugged, as if the collection she just named wasn't completely outrageous.

"What about Jax?" Ardyn couldn't help himself. He had to know what came of the dragon. The last they spoke to Inda, she told them he had shown up and confronted her.

"Yeah, someone gave him an invitation." Her jaw tightened. "It sure as hell wasn't me."

"Good. We can use the firepower." Ardyn attempted to downplay his interest, but it was too late and the comment about fire power only made matters worse.

"As if any old Dragon wouldn't do?" Inda pushed away from the table. "Hell, I'm a phoenix, a bird of fire!"

"Looks like you just joined me on the shit list." Graham slapped Ardyn on the shoulder as Inda stomped away from them. She needed a moment to cool off.

"Looks like it, but I bet I get off the list before you do!" Ardyn jabbed his elbow into Graham's side.

"What's the wager?" Graham pushed him back. "I'll take any bet!"

"Oh, boys, hush. We have incoming." Inda returned to interrupt their building rough housing after a brief moment alone.

CHAPTER 14

Arrival

They **turned to see the wall** that hid the inside of the tunnel as it glowed. Whoever was on the other side was djinn. Inda and Graham could get in and out because Ardyn allowed it. Anyone else would have to be accompanied by another djinn. That was how the barrier worked. It read the signature of their magic. If a djinn wasn't present, anyone else would simply walk into a wall.

"Looks like the first wave has arrived." Graham perked up. "I wonder who this is."

The wall temporarily vanished as the familiar magic became the key to unlock the door. The first to appear was Bruto—the large redheaded djinn—followed by a group that inspired a low hiss and a sneer from Graham. *Slithers*. Ardyn shot the man a look, but Graham pulled his expression together before he could say anything.

"Now this is nice," Bruto boasted as the group filed into the space. "I mean, it's not my ice cave. That's a masterpiece, but I can get used to this." Once everyone was inside, the wall solidified again, and they stood staring at the new members awkwardly.

"Inda, you care to make introductions?" Ardyn nudged her.

"Yes, sorry. Graham, Ardyn, this is Bruto." Bruto bowed and winked at Inda in a way that made her stomach flip. She shook off the feeling. "He's a friend of Jinn. With him is Mike, King of the Slithers, and a few members of his guard." Mike nodded hello. The other slithers stood in formation behind him. Briar's fairy guard had trained them, and they were quick studies. It would be hard to tell that just a matter of weeks prior, they were all living in the slums, just trying to survive.

"Slithers?" Graham sneered. "You've got to be kidding me."

"Yes, what's your problem?" Inda shot Graham a warning look. "Get with the times. Slithers are good now. Remember, they helped save the world."

"Funny, I didn't hear that part of the story." Warning or not, Graham didn't care for the reptilian shifters and he wasn't about to pretend he liked them.

"Of course not," Mike grumbled. He was over the idea of trying to convince everyone else that he and his people were trustworthy. The shit never ended.

"Look, you two are going to have to play nicely here. Remember, we have a lady to save!" Inda said sarcastically.

"Let it go, firebird," Graham poked at her. She'd already talked their ears off about how she felt about Nitara making women look weak. The woman was supposed to be a powerful djinn and yet every time they looked up; a cavalry had to be put together to go save her.

"I'm just saying this is ridiculous. What will she get into next time? Will we all have to come flying to the rescue to clean up her mess again?" Inda had her own hang up, and that was having to run to save Nitara. Time and time again, though she wasn't included on the last effort, but because of the woman, she was about to be forced to share space with the man she'd been skillfully avoiding.

"I sure as hell hope not." Jinn appeared through the barrier with his own passengers, including Jax. "I, for one, am tired of risking my life."

"Jinn, I'm so glad you could make it. I'm Ardyn." The hybrid wolf looked like a groupie as he bound up to the new arrival. "You're, like, a legend." He shot his hand out to Jinn, who looked at it pensively before accepting the handshake.

"Well, thanks, I guess." Jinn shrugged and shot a look at Mike, who was holding back laughter.

"Sorry, I didn't mean to make that weird." Ardyn pulled his hand away and took two unsure steps back from the man.

"Yeah, well, you did." Jax was unable to stop the boisterous sound that rang out as the awkward interaction continued. He winked at his lady (to him she was still just that) and joined Mike, who had walked off to claim a corner.

Mike watched as the rest of the party arrived in well-timed waves. He'd been eager to join the efforts to help Jinn, but the small social bubble he'd retreated to had caused him to forget that not all the world was ready to accept him or his people. He would have to keep fighting, every damn day, to make that happen. Hell, it might not even happen in his lifetime, or his daughter's, but it was a fight he had taken on. It was just exhausting as hell.

"You alright over here?" Jax handed him a beer he grabbed from the bucket that Bruto conjured as he passed by.

"Yeah." Mike cracked open the cold drink and poured half of it down his throat. "I'm fine. Just kinda forgot that the rest of the world still hates me and my people."

"Hate is a strong word. Besides, it's not the rest of the world. Just a select few." Jax pointed to Graham, who'd taken to his own corner. "Hell, the dragons are cool with you. You're basically our reptilian cousins."

"Right, because that's how you always felt." Mike chuckled, but his heart wasn't in it. He hated to admit it, but the not so warm welcome from Graham had really bothered him.

"No, it isn't. I won't lie about that. We thought the same thing about you as everyone else, but what you're overlooking right now is that we changed. We see you for what you are, not as the picture that was painted of you by those who came before you. Hell, trust me, changing the minds of dragons is no simple things. If we can change our perception, so can they." Jax pointed to the vampire, who was finishing a bottle of blood.

"I just hope we can get this shit over with quickly." Mike didn't really care to convince Graham to like him, or any of the other blood suckers. They weren't an issue, considering they never left Reverie. It was just a wake-up call. He still had a lot of work to do for his people.

"Oh, right, so then you can go on your next rescue mission to face the wolves!" Jax teased. "That's the plan, right? Rescue Nitara, so you can head off and find the fae girl?"

"Fuck, I forgot about that. Praia." He took another swig of beer. "This shit is never ending. Jinn is going to want me by his side."

"Considering it was your intel that brought news of her survival, I'm going to say that's a big yes."

"I'm going to need something stronger than beer."

"Hey, you have to stay sober. After all, you're changing the world, one heroic rescue at a time!" Jax laughed and Mike couldn't help but to join in. "Before you know it, the entire world will love you!"

"I'm not sure I'm up for the task." Mike watched the people in the room. Everyone mingled, besides the lone vampire. It was something he thought he would never get to see, his people conversing freely with fairies and dragons without fear of punishment for being out of the Scorched lands.

"Good thing you have all of these people who got your back." Jax put a hand on his shoulder.

"Yeah, you're right. Who would have thought you were such a softy?"

"Hey, dragons, get a bad rep, too!" Jax drew a heart in the air with his fingers and pouted.

"I guess so." Mike laughed once more before their attention was drawn to the entrance again.

The wall shimmered as the last of their group arrived. Rosie had to make a grand entrance. The curvy djinn with a neon pink signature to her magic waltzed in as if she were being announced at a ball. She sauntered across the threshold, which remained open just long enough for the rest of the fairies accompanying her to walk in.

"Okay, if we're all staying here, I'm going to have to expand on the space." Ardyn eyed the wall that stood opposite the entrance. He'd put it in place to define the space, but behind it were miles of more tunnels. "I wasn't expecting so many people." He waved a hand at the black wall, and in a move that looked effortless, he pushed it back, deeper into the tunnel, and as it did, individual rooms appeared. "Figured you all might want some privacy at some point. Each room has a shower as well. There should be enough for everyone here."

"Now, this is proper accommodations. Don't you think so, dragon boy?" Rosie poked at Jax. The last time they met, she'd been complaining about the guest quarters the dragons had set up for the group that visited his home. No matter how many times he told her that it wasn't really where they hosted guests, she ignored him and complained further about the cots they had the nerve to call proper bedding.

Jax shook his head. There was no point in engaging with her on the topic again. She would only continue to complain about something that, in the end, had nothing to do with him. Instead, he headed off to choose a room for himself before all the good ones were claimed.

"You sure you have enough space for all of us?" Jinn looked around; there were forty members in their group.

"Yep! And if not, these tunnels go on for miles. I can always create more." Grinning proudly, Ardyn waved his hand around in a display that worked up some of his magic that danced in a green flame around his fingers.

"Make sure you keep that trigger finger at ease," Briar chimed in. "They have sensors out."

"What?" Ardyn dropped his hand and his flame when out.

"I noticed them on the way in. It's Fae magic, at least it's based on the design. If a large influx of magic is sensed in the area, it will alert them." She peered over a few maps that were laid out on the table. "I'm sure it's the same that was used after the war between the two sides. It's likely how they make sure the vamps aren't stirring up too much shit. However, the ones I saw were modified. They're set to detect all kinds of magic."

"I didn't see anything like that." Ardyn went to his screen.

"Yeah, they're hard to spot. But if you know what to look for ..." Briar pointed to the map. "There! There is a tree along this grove. It's one of the sensors."

"How can you know that?" He pulled up the location on the screen and zoomed in on the tree line she indicated. When she spotted the one in question, she had him isolate the image.

"Look at the way the branches bend, to make a pattern. It's a trigger point. Not far from here either, so I'd be careful."

"We need to scout for more of these." Jinn watched over Briar's shoulder. "There's no telling how many there are."

"I'll go," Inda offered. "They won't be surprised to see me out there since I've been around here for a while now."

"I'll join you." Graham stepped up. "I could use the fresh air."

"Are you sure that's a good idea? Sarah is looking for you." Inda knew why she wanted out, to get away from the dragon, but Graham leaving would be a risk for them.

"Yeah, I'm sure. I'll keep a low profile," he assured her, but she was still suspicious of his motives.

"Right, okay." Ardyn wasn't sure it was a great idea, but he wouldn't argue. He could tell that Graham was struggling with being near Mike and the other slithers. He had no idea why; the man had never shown any prejudice toward any other kind before.

"Great, glad to have such eager volunteers." Smiling, Briar waved for the two to come over. She pointed at the screen. "This is what you're looking for. It may be subtler on other trees, it may just be a branding on a stone, so be very careful." She looked at her friend. "You will have to pay close attention to your surroundings while you're out there. If you can, just take note of them from the air and keep moving. Your magic is a lot different from the vampires and it may trigger them. Graham should be okay but keep an eye out for anyone that may be on patrol if she is indeed looking for you."

"Anything else we should know?" Graham asked as the map vanished from the screen.

"There may be a slight variation in the design, depending on what they are out for. I wouldn't be surprised if they have been changed specifically for you if you're a person of interest. In that case, I suggest you keep alert and keep your distance. Move as quickly as you can."

"Right, got it." Graham turned and headed for the exit.

CHAPTER 15

Bunker

A*rdyn began helping everyone get* settled into their new rooms. Unexpectedly, the groups didn't take to collective corners. Everyone was intermingled. Having gone on a similar mission together, they'd learn to make friends. For some, it was a joyful reunion with people they otherwise wouldn't see. Over time, the Earth had benefited from the new order of things, but its inhabitants hadn't. They'd become segregated and hostile toward one another, even those that were once allies.

"Inda tells me it took some convincing to get you here." Ardyn approached Jinn, who was looking over maps of the vampire territory.

"Is that so?" He kept his eyes trained on the paper, memorizing the perimeter lines.

"Yeah, and I don't mean to be intrusive, but I'm moved to ask you why that was." When Jinn didn't respond to his implied question, he went on. "I mean, Nitara is a great woman, or at least she has always been to me. I guess I'm just wondering what would make you turn your back on her."

"Turn my back on her?" Jinn huffed. "You know, you're real bold to come to me with that. Look, I didn't turn my back on her. I was there for her; I always have been. She is the one who turned her back on me."

"But now that you know that she didn't want to do it, that she had no choice, you're back on her side?" Ardyn pressed. He'd already crossed the line, might as well go for the gold.

"I was never not on her side!" Jinn's voice echoed, creating a hush that covered the entire compound. "Every day I searched for her, I fought Daegal for her, I battled next to dragons for her! And after everything was said and done, she turned her back on me! She walked away from me! Yet no one seems to remember that part."

"She had a good reason." Ardyn regretted his decision to approach Jinn with the topic.

"You say that now, that she had a good reason." Jinn stepped closer to him. "But perhaps you can answer something for me that no one else seems to be able to. If she cared so much about me, about us as a couple, why couldn't she tell me about any of this? And don't give me that bull about what Daegal did or the consequences. There is nothing in this world that Nitara can't share with me, and she knows that. She could have had faith in me, and that we would figure this shit out together. But she didn't. She walked away, she took the easy way out and yet every fucking person is in *my* face as if I am the one who did something wrong. Do me a favor and back the hell off. Nitara needs help, and I'm here. I didn't promise anyone fuzzy feelings and some grand emotional rediscovery!" Jinn shoved Ardyn out of his way as he headed to claim his own room.

"Well, I could have told you that was a bad idea." Rosie materialized next to Ardyn and hopped on the table. Crossing her legs, she allowed a shoe to dangle from her toe.

"I didn't mean to upset him." Ardyn took his eyes off the back of Jinn, who was walking away from them.

"Didn't you though?" She raised a brow. "You were testing him to see where his loyalty really lies, and you figured out what you wanted. Any fool could see that asking him anything about Nitara right now was going to push him over the edge."

"Perhaps you're right."

"Ain't no perhaps about it, baby." She smiled knowingly. "But you keep telling yourself whatever you need to if it helps you make it through this."

Inda and Graham returned to a quiet tunnel. Everyone inside had remained in their quarters. After Jinn's outburst, it was a collective agreement to keep the noise to a minimum. When the entrance shimmered, announcing their arrival, they were met by Briar and Ardyn. Jinn remained in hiding. He needed the time to meditate.

"It's a fucking minefield out there, and there are more the closer we get to the city," Graham reported to the greeting party.

"Yes, I counted nine on my half, and that's just the trees. Some of the stones looked like they may have had markings, but I couldn't get close enough to tell," Inda confirmed.

"Yeah, the things are everywhere and that's just here. Who knows how many are in the city or around their home?" Graham was relieved to find that Mike wasn't there. "Knowing Sarah, the place is probably covered in them."

"The good thing is that we know they are here, and we know what to look for." Briar's mind was already spinning. There had to be a way around them, some way to neutralize the alarms. "This gives us an upper hand."

"Yeah, but how do we avoid triggering them?" Inda took a seat next to the table, and the others joined her as they brainstormed for their next move.

Briar picked up the printed image of the tree she first saw. "It looks like these are of a weaker design. Without fae magic to reinforce them, their perimeter won't be that wide. I suggest we test one." Briar pointed to a spot on the opposite side of the map from their current location. "Find one farther away from here and see how close we have to be to trigger it. They will start to glow when they are set off. At least this way we know what we're up against, and we can divert their attention elsewhere. While they are looking over there, we can be working over here to get things in order."

"Sounds like a plan. Who's up for the task?" Inda asked for volunteers.

"You can count me in!" Jax stepped up from the small group that joined them, including Mike, who had been avoiding the vampire in the room. Inda flinched and cursed herself for making it optional. With all eyes plastered on her, she had no choice but to accept his offer of help.

"Fine, let's go. But try not to be seen."

"That won't be a problem." A small fairy, nicknamed Bunny for the bounce in her step, pushed to the front of the group. "I've given everyone here a cloaking spell. It shouldn't be enough magic to set off the wards unless you're right on top of one."

"Good. Looks like we've thought of everything." Inda wanted a reason to postpone the trip, any reason at all, but she wouldn't be getting one. "Let's get out of here."

"Good luck." Mike jabbed Jax in the ribs. The man was in for hell with her.

Outside of the wall, the sky was bright, which meant they would have free room to roam. The vampires would be down for the count, and their human watchdogs wouldn't be able to catch sight of the dragon with his cloak. Jax stretched his limbs as he prepared to shift again. He took his time and watched the woman, who avoided returning the look.

"Are you ever going to talk to me, Inda?" He couldn't take it anymore. The silence from her was more painful than her being away from him.

"When I have something to say, yes, I'll talk." She stretched her neck and tried to ease the tightness in her shoulders. "Until then, no, I don't think I will."

"All this time, and you have nothing to say to me." Jax walked away from the entrance and out into the open field. He turned back to her with a sorrowful expression. "I have a million words. My heart is bursting with anger, and confusion … and love. Yet you have nothing to say." Before she could respond, Jax spread his wings and took to the sky.

Inda watched him flying for a moment, and the tightness in her shoulders extended to the center of her chest. Before the tear could fall, the phoenix took flight.

"Are you going to tell me what the hell is going on with you?" Ardyn cornered Graham, who was headed to his room beneath the ground. The sun was up, and though he was hidden from it, the effects were still just as strong. Mike had created him a special room to keep him away from the noise of everyone else who would be wide awake. "I've never known you to have a problem with anyone unless the reason was valid. Not even really with the bastards who turned their back on you and accepted Tyrellis as their leader. Yet now it seems you can't even look at Mike without snapping or sneering. You want to tell me what's the problem is there?"

"You know, there was a time in my life when I was happy. Completely and totally in a way that it took centuries to accomplish." He eyed the group of slithers that headed down the hall toward their rooms. "I had a part of my life that I protected just as fiercely as everyone here is trying to protect Nitara. You don't get to live as long as I have without finding someone to share your time with, without building real, solid relationships. I had that at one time. I had that, and it was the best thing in my world. But you know when the wars broke out, and the slithers decided to play on both sides of the fence, I lost that. They took away from me the one person who I would give up the world for

.

"They stole from me that eternity of peace and love wrapped inside of a person who judged me for nothing and wanted nothing more than to be with me. Every damn day I think about her and the fact that I will never get to have her in my life again. And now I'm supposed to buddy up with one of the things that stole my love away from me?" Graham swallowed the anger rising from within. He wouldn't be friends, he wouldn't play along with what everyone else wanted, but he also wouldn't start any shit. Graham was smart enough to know better. They outnumbered him. If anything was to jump off, the people there would no doubt choose Mike over the vampire they'd only just met.

"Graham, I'm sorry. I didn't know that you were going through that. You never shared with me anything about your past. I had no idea." Ardyn had intended to chew the man out for his behavior, but he hadn't expected to hear of a lost love, or of the pain that Graham was suffering.

"Yeah, well, some things are meant to be known by the entire world and some things we keep to ourselves because they're so hard to share. They're two difficult to breathe life to and have to hash out repeatedly." Graham reached for the door that led to his isolated room. "Look, I'm down for this fight. I want more than anything to get Nitara out of the hell she's in, and to free my people from the bastard who claims to be leading us to a better place. But you can forget wanting me and Mike or any of his slithering family to ever become friends. Because, as far as I see it, he is the enemy. They are the enemy."

"So, you mean to tell me you will hold him responsible for actions and decisions that were not his own? Mike wasn't there, and neither were any of his guards. Hell, if they were, you would have ripped their heads off the moment they walked in here. They had nothing to do with what happened to your girl."

Ardyn couldn't believe what he was hearing. He always thought so highly of Graham because he kept to himself and never got involved with any of the vampire drama going on around them. He thought the man was progressive and understanding, but what he just said proved that Ardyn didn't know Graham as well as he thought he did.

"Yeah, well, see me about that when wolves become friends with the vampires because not all of us want to drink their blood." Graham kept his hand on the door, ready to escape the conversation. He knew Ardyn wasn't finished.

"Did you forget that I'm a wolf? Yeah, I'm different now but I'm still a wolf, and as far as I know, me and you are cool, but you can let me know if I'm wrong on that point." Ardyn walked away from Graham, no longer wanting to carry on the conversation about which species won the award for being the worst. They all had their shit to bear. There was no clean race of supernatural beings. Every one of them had taken lives and destroyed futures, but they all deserved a clean slate.

They all deserved the opportunity to do better than the ones before them. If Graham was so hell-bent on holding his grudge, perhaps he wasn't the right leader for the vampires. What made him any better than the monster currently leading them? As hard as it was for Ardyn to think that Graham wouldn't be right, he knew the alternative was much worse.

CHAPTER 16

Breaking Tyrellis

"You know, Nitara really has** a way of getting you men all wrapped around her little finger." Rosie walked into the room that Jinn had claimed for his own. She waited patiently for him to end his meditation. It was important for Jinn, the only way he kept from flying off the handle. "I really need to take a few notes from that girl."

"What do you want?" He was in no mood to discuss his feelings about Nitara again. It was all anyone wanted to do. And of course, just moments after he'd found himself as close to peace as he would be able to get, there was Rosie, ready and willing to shake shit up again.

"I just came to check on you. I overheard that conversation between you and the weird one." She sat in the chair next to the door. "What's up with him? Half wolf, half djinn. Daegal really got into some weird shit, huh?"

"Oh, did you?" He threw a towel over his shoulder, showing that he intended to head for the shower, but Rosie ignored the cue. "I don't know anything about him, but he seems to think he knows a lot about me."

"Interesting how that works out, isn't it? Well, if you ask me, he has a thing for your girl." Rosie was great at pushing Jinn's buttons, but unlike those around her, she knew which ones to push and when to push them. Jinn was a special sort of man who needed to be nudged in the right direction. Everyone else was coming at him with a battering ram.

"What else is new?" Jinn was used to it. Nitara had a certain allure that made most men want her. She was confident, a little cocky, and a ball buster. Men liked that. She was also soft and seductive, and men loved that.

"It doesn't bother you?"

"Not as much as this conversation is starting to." Jinn knew Rosie just as well as she knew him. The woman was playing an angle, and he needed to figure out what it was.

"Okay, so topic change?" she offered a bit too readily.

"Please." He tossed the towel on the bed. She wasn't going away anytime soon.

"To be honest, I'm not sure what the hell else we're supposed to be talking about here, considering our overall objective is to save she who shall not be named." She looked at the door and back at Jinn. "But I'm bored and everyone out there is a snooze fest."

"We could talk about you and Bruto." Grinning, he sat on the bed. Finally, someone else's love life could be on the table.

"There is nothing to talk about." She shrugged and delivered the standard response.

"Oh, please." He'd had enough of everyone in his business but not reciprocating on the newsfeed. "The two of you disappeared together right after all that shit was done in the Cascades. When I got back, both of you had vanished in a mix of pink and orange smoke, and no one has heard from either of you. And now, I call Bruto for help, not him, but both of you arrive together. You expect me to believe nothing is going on there?"

"I expect you to mind your business," she warned playfully.

"Ah, see, I'm the one who has to mind my business, yet all of my personal info is supposed to be on grand display for all to see? You think that's fair?"

"Okay, I'll give you something if you give me something." Rosie raised a brow. She knew she had him; she was sitting on info that Jinn had wanted for about as long as she knew him.

"Okay, deal." It was too good to pass up. For years he had wondered what the hell went on between the two of them and now he had a chance to find out what it was.

"Bruto and I have, for a while now, had an off-and-on fling. From time to time, we hook up. It's familiar, nice, and safe. I know that despite how crude the man can be, Bruto won't hurt me. He is careful with me and my heart. No, it's no fairy tale love, but hell, I've had two or three of those now and trust me when I say they are so fucking overrated." She let it sink in, the confirmation that the world wanted but never got.

"Wow, I never thought I would see the day when either of you admitted to it." He'd always known that something was going on between them, but he figured he'd be in the dark about it forever. "It's weird, knowing the truth, but now I have so many more questions."

"Yeah, well you have, and hell has frozen over, so you're welcome." She winked. "And you got the one answer you bargained for. Keep the follow-ups to yourself."

"Ha! Thanks." Jinn considered trying to push for more info, but considering how long it took to get that tidbit, his hopes weren't high for much more.

"Okay, now it's your turn. Spill."

"What is it you want to know?" He made the deal and now he would have to own up to it. He was pretty sure what the question would be.

"I want to know what's the deal. All this time, you've never faltered when it came to Nitara. Since I've known you, you have gone to the ends of the world and back for that woman, but now you're all shaken." She paused. "Keep in mind that I'm not asking to be nosey or to figure out if you still love her, because I know that you do. I'm asking this because you are my friend Jinn, and I'm genuinely concerned and worried about you. What's going on?"

"After what you just said, I'd think you'd have no problem understanding." Dropping his head back, he stared at the ceiling for a moment before he gave her the answer she wanted. "Nitara walked away from me. She told me her heart belonged to someone else, and she vanished. I didn't get one-word in. As you said, I went to the ends of the Earth for that woman and all I got in return were a few weak ass words that were barely an apology or a thank you and she was gone. Just like that." He found the face of his friend and chose to confide in her, because he knew that no one else would understand. "Don't get me wrong. I'm glad now to find out that it wasn't exactly what I thought it was, but that still hurt. And what's saying that after all this, we save her, and she's free of whatever spell Daegal burdened her with, that she will really want to be with me? Who's saying that Ardyn or Graham, or one of the hundreds of other guys who would come banging down her door, isn't who she really wants? Everyone keeps asking me to risk it all for her but fail to recall that the last time I did that, I came up empty. I have nothing left to risk. What happens this time?"

"Jinn, baby, I'm so sorry. I had no idea you felt that way." Rosie lost all the sass from her tone, and for a moment, she was just his friend, no gimmick or mask necessary. "Why didn't you talk to me?"

"I was too busy confiding in the bottle." He shrugged. "Also, you were off with Bruto." He couldn't help it. He had to take the jab.

"Well, for what it's worth, and I suspect it isn't much, I don't think that she would turn from you. If she didn't have a real absolute reason to do so. There is no way that Nitara wouldn't want to be by your side." She shuddered. "I can't imagine what she is going through now. Trapped inside of a fucking vampire. Man, my little jewelry box was hard enough, but who knows what it's like in there."

"It's hell." Jinn didn't have to imagine it. He knew exactly what Nitara was going through.

"Oh, that's right, you've been there ... sort of."

"Yeah, and she isn't doing well." It hurt Jinn to think of his wife, the woman he loved, trapped inside that hell. It hurt even more that he continued to think of her in that way.

"All the more reason for us to stop moping around and get her out of there. Regardless of what happens when she is free, she is still one of us and we protect our own." Rosie wouldn't allow it to be any other way. The djinn were her family, the only one she would ever have.

The surrounding walls shook. It made no sense, but they did. She felt boxed in, and with every labored breath he took, the trembles began again. The life, that sad echo of what once was, faded and was harder to hear with each passing moment. She called out to Tyrellis, but it made no difference. No amount of noise reached him. He was gone, his mind too far away from her reaches. There was another tremble just like before, but this time it was accompanied by crumbling. The walls grayed, and as they did, pieces fell to the floor and turned to ash. They were killing him, and with him, she would parish. Nitara curled in on herself, and for the first time in many years, she said a prayer that someone would come. The echo of voices reached her. She could actually hear them talking outside of his body.

"Good, keep it up. We must continue to drain him." Sarah's voice was sickening.

"What about Cast? Isn't he supposed to challenge Tyrellis? If we drain all the blood from him, how will he do that?" a woman questioned. She had a familiar trill to her tone. It was one that she heard before, and it wasn't from a vampire.

"Cast will make no such challenge." Sarah's heels smacked against the floor as she walked away. She paused. "Make sure there is nothing left of him. I don't want him returning. Or that bitch trapped inside."

Nitara was shocked, but more so angered. Sarah knew exactly what she was doing. With Tyrellis trapped and drained, he would remain unable to release Nitara. It wasn't enough just to kill Tyrellis, but she wanted Nitara to suffer right along with him. The more he dried up, the more his mind slowed down. The silence was so much more maddening than what was once ranting and continued begging. Nitara pulled herself to her feet and tried yet again to use her magic, anything to free herself or bring some life back to the man. She called her weapon of choice, her whip, to her hand and focused on the spot that was usually her way out. With everything she had, she pulled the whip back and snapped it forward. The tip of the string of light smacked into the barrier that stood between her and freedom. In an explosion of purple light, the magic that she pushed out bounced back against her and knocked her on her ass. The already fragile surroundings crumbled even further.

Nitara pulled herself up and brushed the debris from her hair. She wasn't going to get out of there, not on her own. As a last-ditch effort, she tried to reach out to the one person she could, to the person who she couldn't believe was still on her side.

"Jinn, if you're out there, if you can hear me please say something," Nitara spoke into the darkness and waited. She wanted to call out again, but before her lips parted, she received a response.

"Yes, Nitara, I'm here." Jinn's voice returned to her, but it hurt her to hear it. He sounded tired, frustrated, and upset—and she knew it was because of her.

"It's so good to hear your voice ... or any voice, for that matter." She meant it. Despite the anguish in his tone, she was happy to know that he was still there, on the other side, open to her.

"What's going on?" Jinn could tell by her voice that Nitara was struggling. "Are you okay? How are you holding up in there?"

"I wish I could say that I was doing great, but that would be a lie. They're torturing him, and it's affecting me. I'm getting weaker with every moment. I'm surprised that I could reach you at all."

"I'm glad that you did. Listen to me. I know you are tired, but I need you to tell me what's going on. I need to know everything. Nitara, leave nothing out."

"It's just becoming too quiet; they're draining his body and it's slowing him down. I can't feel him here anymore, and I don't know how much longer I can take this. I feel like I'm losing my mind in here. It's not the same. It's not the same as being inside of a vase or a bottle. Those things are inanimate objects and they don't respond to us. They don't feel us the way he feels me. I feel him, too, Jinn. And I feel everything he's going through; I hear everything he thinks in my mind. He's stopping, he's slowing down, and I feel like the same thing is happening to me. I don't know how much longer I'll be here. I don't know what happens to me. If he stops, if he dies, so do I."

"We're not going to let that happen, Nitara," Jinn promised her. "We're going to get you out of there."

CHAPTER 17

Time to move

"**All right, we need to** get this shit moving." Jinn entered the hub and shocked everyone there. He'd been hidden away for so long, they wondered if he would ever come out of his room again. "Our timeline has just been shifted forward. We don't have time for days of planning. We need to get in and get her out of there. Now."

"Jinn?" Briar stood from the round table, a recent addition to the space. "What's going on?"

"Nitara contacted me." He pulled on the leather jacket that had been dangling in his hand. "She's not holding up well, and we need to do something now. She's fading."

"How?" Ardyn abandoned his seat as well.

"That is not really the concern right now." Jinn shot him a warning look. The man had already crossed the line with him once.

"You're right. What did she say?" Ardyn looked hurt, but backed down. Jinn was older and stronger, and he didn't want to piss him off.

"They're torturing Tyrellis. Sounds like they're draining his body. But whatever they are doing to him is affecting her as well." He thought about what she said. "It's not the normal process. I've seen vamps drained before, and they just enter a typical sleep, but this sounds like they are killing him, in a slow and painful way."

"Nitara is still safe. That's good, right?" Briar hung on to the one bit of good news he had for them.

"Yes, but she sounds bad. I don't think we have much time." Jinn looked at the screen, which flashed to an image of the oversized home of the vampire leader. "We need to get in there. What's the best way?"

"I guess a sneaky infiltration won't work." Mike stared at the map on the table.

"Maybe it is." Ardyn's eyes lit up as his mind went to work.

"What do you mean?" Jinn questioned him and followed his gaze to the map, where he pointed.

"Hell, we've scouted out these damn magic traps. We know where they are. Let's say we set them off all over the place. Sarah will think she is being attacked and will have no choice but to send her people out to investigate. While they're doing that, we can walk right in."

"Even if she sends people, she won't send them all, and the ones that go, won't be gone for long," Inda offered.

"How long do you think we'll have before they realize it's a setup?" Jinn questioned Ardyn, who worked quickly to calculate the timing in his head.

"Not long at all, a matter of minutes. I say we'd have to be in and out within twenty minutes, tops. Anything longer than that and we'll be trapped. I don't know what defenses she has, but I know she is working with someone who possesses magic. None of this would happen if she wasn't."

"That's good enough for me."

"So, we're snatching his body and running?" Mike lifted his gaze from the map. "Is that the plan now?"

"I don't see what other choice we have right now." Briar joined Jinn in scrutinizing the picture on the screen. "Twenty minutes isn't going to be enough time to revive him if they've drained him. We'd have to first try to revive him and then figure out how to get Nitara out. We won't be able to do what we need to until we get some life back into him. Don't forget, they also have some sort of magical binding around him. I'm confident that we'll be able to get through it, but it might take some time."

"All right. Plans have changed. We're kidnapping a half dead vampire vessel!" Bruto perked up. "This is my kind of action!"

"Boxi, you and the others start creating the magical bombs. They can be placed in the zones and set off from afar. This way, we don't risk our people having a run-in with any hungry vamps. We want to get out of here as clean as possible."

Boxi nodded and left the room to prepare the others.

"While they're doing that, we need to rally the groups. Have everyone line up to have the cloaking reinforced. We want to make sure everyone stays safe out there." Briar took to running the show. The men were too much of a mess to do anything right. Jinn was stuck in his head, Mike was stuck in his feelings, and she didn't know what the hell was up with Ardyn. Just as she finished issuing her orders, Graham appeared from his hidden space.

"Okay, I'll get my people in order." Mike stood from the table, happy to have a reason to get away from the vampire, but when he turned to leave, Graham was in his way. Instead of stepping aside to allow Mike room to get by, Graham slammed his shoulder into him.

"What the hell is your problem?" Mike pushed Graham back.

"My problem is you." Graham issued another blow that knocked Mike back into the table. "You and your bottom feeding friends!"

"That's it. I'm sick of your shit. You wanna go, let's go!" Mike had had enough. There were only so many times that he could allow himself to be challenged or pushed in front of his people without standing up for himself. Graham had done nothing but test his resolve since he arrived.

Graham was thrilled and launched a powerful blow at Mike's jaw. He was sure it would knock him out, but Mike's skin changed, taking on the malleable properties of his snake, and absorbed the blow before he launched one right back at Graham. The vampire slid back and hit the table behind him. Mike pounced and was on top of him. They launched repeated shots at each other and tumbled around the room.

"Enough!" Jinn yelled so loudly that the room trembled, and dust fell from the ceiling. Everyone in the room froze. "I didn't come all of this way to see two grown ass men act like children. You two got issues, handle it, but on your own time. This isn't your time. This is *my* time. So suck it up! Mike, get your people ready. Graham, whatever you need to do to get your head focused on the task at hand, do it! We don't have time for this shit."

Mike straightened himself out and wiped the blood from his lip. He looked back at Graham, pleased to see that he, too, had shed some blood. With a satisfied grin, he headed off down the hall. Briar followed him closely.

"Mike, are you okay?" She touched him on the shoulder to stop him when they were out of view of the others.

"No, I'm sick of this shit." He turned to face her. "I feel like a damn fool! I let myself believe it was possible for us to move forward. But here we are dealing with the same bullshit. Despite the fact that there are bigger issues to be concerned with, this man is so blinded by his hatred for my people that he can't get past it and allow us to work together for the greater good. What the hell am I supposed to do with that?"

"You can't let him disrupt what you've already done. You've made such significant progress. That needs to be the focus here."

"Have I?" Glancing down at the blood on his hand, he smirked, knowing that it was not his own.

"Are you telling me you have doubts about that? Look at your people. Look at how you've rebuilt. That is what matters, Mike. Not him or anyone else who can't let go of the past. You and your people need to be worried about restoring the bond between you. Only then will the outside world ever see you as anything other than the traitors that they've been taught to view you as."

"Focus on our own, huh?" Funny that she was saying that while he and his people were once again risking everything for someone else.

"Look around. That is what everyone else does. They don't worry about other people. We don't either. We build ourselves up first before we ever worry about what someone else thinks. You, at least, are doing that in a positive way. The world will see it. And hell, if they don't, fuck them. You have the fairy, the fae, the djinn, and the dragons, all on your side. If you ask me, that's one hell of an alliance."

"Thank you, Briar."

"Yeah, no problem. Now suck it up so we can go save Nitara."

"Again," they both said in unison and laughed as they went to talk to their people.

"You think we're going to be able to get through this without any drama?" Bruto joined Jinn and handed him a mug of coffee, spiked with Irish cream. It was a favorite and one that always helped his friend relax.

"Hell no!" He laughed. "Look around. This place is full of little drama bombs. You have the fire bird and her ex dragon. Then there is the vampire who has it out for the reptile. And don't forget the wolf hybrid who's in love with Nitara. Man, shit is going to hit the fan, hard."

"Well, I can say it's always a great time when we get together!" Bruto slapped his shoulder and tossed back the rest of his drink. "Care for something a little stronger?" He shook the empty glass at Jinn.

"Believe it or not, I think I've had my fill. Besides, I need to keep my head clear for tomorrow."

"Yeah, that's probably for the best." Bruto tapped his own cup, which refilled. Jinn lifted a brow at him. "What? I work better with a buzz!"

The flares went off as planned. Jinn hid outside of the vampire home with Mike, Bruto, and Ardyn. When the vampires started to leave, running to check the alarms that had been set off, they all made a run for it. Getting inside was easy, almost too easy, but they were in. Ardyn had managed to design another bug, one that worked more with technology than magic. It went in ahead of them and mapped out the path to Tyrellis' holding cell. The cloak worked to get them close to the house, but the moment they crossed the threshold, there would be no hiding.

As they headed inside, Briar, Rosie, Graham, and Jax took their positions outside. It would be their task, along with the cloaked slithers who blended in with the lush gardens that surrounded the home, to keep any returning vampires at bay. They needed to give Jinn and the others as much time as they could on the inside. The paths back to the home were loaded with traps and members of the team who were ready to fight at all costs.

"It looks like we have quite a bit of a maze to work through." Ardyn held up the tablet that displayed the map the bug had laid out. "She's deep within the center of the home."

"Can you just flash us there?" Graham questioned. "I mean, there are three djinn here, and hell, once we're in, like you said, the jig is up anyway."

"He has a point." Bruto shrugged. "Let's fast track this, shall we?" He laid his hand on Mike's shoulder and the two vanished in a flash of light.

"Onward!" Ardyn smiled, took hold of Graham, and they disappeared.

Jinn glanced up at the open balcony and the bird of fire who was coming in for a landing. He wished Inda luck with her part of the play before he vanished in a cloud of blue to join the others.

__You really are a cold__ bitch, you know that?" Red boots touched down on the white marble floor of the open balcony. Inda put out her flames and walked through the sheer curtains that danced in the cool air. Sarah sat in the chair and brushed her hair at the gothic style vanity. Even with the visitor, she remained cool, grooming herself as if the world wasn't about to burn all around her.

"Am I to be concerned with your opinion of me?" Her eyes were trained on the reflection of herself as she primped and preened.

"Maybe not, but you should be concerned with all the shit that is going on in your home right now."

"Oh, should I?" She turned in the chair. "Tell me, what's going on that I should be so concerned with?"

"Your little plan for Cassius to take over. It will not work." Inda stood in the center of the room surrounded by frill. She wanted to gag; Sarah was such a stereotype.

"What would make you think that I want Cassius to be in charge?" The vampire slid her bare feet into a pair of heeled slippers, the kind with fur around the toes. "Cassius has no place at the head of a nation. He's a baby."

"You only set him up for the throne," Inda barked. "You took out Tyrellis and lined him up for a direct path to where he wants to be. Now you claim to not want that? Do you deny helping him?"

"Everything you say is true, except I didn't help Cassius. He helped me. Right now, our little friend is down there, fighting, and failing to keep a throne that isn't even his yet." She grabbed the robe that hung on the wall next to her, tied it around her waist, and walked over to Inda. The two stood just a few feet apart, and neither flinched. "What do you suppose will happen then? Once two men have fallen, and the only other person who is even knowledgeable of what it takes to run this place is ...?"

"You." Inda nodded in almost admiration. "You want it for yourself."

"I deserve it! Hell, I've been running this place for years. Tyrellis does nothing but sit around and pout. He just wasted a wonderful gift that was given to him! Nitara could have been used to bring us to greatness and all he did was wish for ridiculous decorations and extended nights. We should be better than this. With a djinn on our side, we should be so much greater!"

"And you think you can make that happen? You think you can bring your people to greatness?" Inda shook her head. "The fae would never allow it."

"Oh, I know I can! Because while my husband was making his silly little wishes, I was making allies. Allies who are now working to stop your brave little band of people from getting what they want." She shrugged. "And the fae won't be a problem for me. This time, we'll be ready for a fight, and it won't be some simple little battle, it will be an all-out war!"

"What?" Inda's fist tightened at her side. "What the hell are you talking about? You want to start a war with the fae?"

"Yes, that is exactly what I want. And tonight will be the spark that ignites the flame." Sarah rolled her shoulders and licked her lips hungrily. "We saw you coming, all of you, and none of you will ever leave!"

"Fuck." Inda burst into flames and burned the woman, who lunged for her. She ran for the open doors that led out to the balcony and took to the sky; she barely escaped the second attack but ran headfirst into oncoming fire. Down below, the vampires were back, and there was an ongoing battle on the front lawn. From above, the dragons swooped in and created a wall of fire between them and their enemy. Inda headed inside and find Jinn. She had to warn them they were walking into a trap.

*"**What the hell is that** sound?"* Ardyn covered his ears. His wolf's sense picked up the noise before theirs could.

"I don't hear anything." Mike listened closely, but was met with silence.

"Something isn't right. We need to get out of here." Ardyn started to pace the floor. They had walked into a trap. He hadn't figured out how, but he knew it.

"Not before we have her." Jinn looked at the room that held Tyrellis' body. It was protected by a barrier, a strong one that he hadn't figured out how to get around. "This is fae magic. Why is there fae magic here?"

"Briar said they adopted the alarms. Maybe this is another one they made their own." Mike touched the barrier and pulled his hand back as the flesh on his finger sizzled. "Fuck, that burns!"

"We don't have time for this, guys," Ardyn warned. "Whatever the hell this is, it's getting louder and closer."

"Oh, fuck it!" Bruto stepped back as far as he could get, and his body lit up with orange light. He pressed his left foot back against the wall to give him more leverage and force behind his charge. He kicked off and ran head-on at the barrier. As he ran, blue light joined orange to add another layer of protection; Jinn was projecting his energy on to Bruto. Quickly, Ardyn mimicked the move. With the combined power, Bruto shattered the barrier on impact. He fell to the ground. "Well, that was unpleasant."

"Yeah, but it worked!" Jinn smiled as he stepped forward without issue.

"That was badass!" Mike gave him a hand to lift him from the ground.

"Good, now grab the body and let's get the hell out of here." Ardyn seemed more panicked than ever. He walked over to the body and carefully examined it before touching anything. "Shit, it's on a sensor."

"What does that mean?" Bruto dusted himself off.

"It means if we move him, it's going to trigger something." Jinn hunched down to examine the setup. "We need to figure out what it is."

"Might it have something to do with this little wire that is digging into his temple?" Mike pointed to the small wire that connected to the base of the bed. He followed the wire to the base of the bed, where a charge for an explosive was set.

"She has his brain connected to a pressure point? That is just sick!" Bruto moved forward to get a closer look. "Lucky for us, I know how to get around this."

"You do? How?" Mike asked as Ardyn went to the entrance to check for the source of the approaching noise.

"Let's just say I spent a lot of time around wars and leave it at that." He winked. Bruto's past was a dark one, but he'd never get into it with anyone else.

"Okay, how much time do you need?" Jinn questioned.

"A few minutes. I'll have to disconnect the sensor and trick it at the same time. We're going to all have to pop out of here together."

"Good, get it done."

"Guys, I don't think we have that much time!" Down the hall he could see them—vampires ran toward them, but something was off. It was something in their eyes. It took him another moment to realize what it was. *Blood lust.* "We've got newborns!"

"What?" Bruto turned to him.

"Focus!" Jinn joined Ardyn at the door. "Shit, this bitch has created newborn vampires to do her dirty work! We have to keep them at bay!"

Jinn and Ardyn threw wave after wave of fire down the hall and burned the vampires alive. It was working until Ardyn looked out of the corner of his eyes and saw more coming from the opposite end of the hall. "Jinn, I think we're going to need a new plan!"

"Get back!" Jinn shot a stream of energy up into the ceiling. The hallway caved in. "Bruto, get it done! That will buy us some time, but not much!"

"Just … one … more … second … Done!" Bruto held the wire in his hand. "Okay, we'll have about six seconds to get our asses out of here before this thing does whatever the hell it's meant to do."

"Good, let's go!" Jinn and Ardyn joined them by Tyrellis. "We have to do this at the same time, if one person shifts a second before the rest of us, his mind is toast!"

"Okay, count us down." Jinn ordered and Bruto started his count at ten seconds. Before he could get to three, they were interrupted.

"Where the hell do you think you're going?" Cassius strolled into the room. He looked at the state of Tyrellis' body and was shocked, but shook it off.

"We don't have time for this, man!" Graham yelled and Bruto continued to count.

"Go." Mike stepped away from the bed.

"What the hell are you doing?" Ardyn questioned him and shot a look at Jinn, who kept his eyes trained on the stiff vampire.

"Get her out of here!" Mike lunged at Cassius, and shifted mid leap into an alligator, as Bruto's count reached zero and the others disappeared.

CHAPTER 18

Everyone Gets Out

"**We have to go back** for him!" Briar yelled at Jinn and slammed her fist on the table. "Why did you let him do that?"

"Let him? We didn't *let* him do anything," Bruto interjected. Briar was out of line. "Mike made that decision on his own. No one made him. I'm not even sure why he felt the need to do that. We were nearly out of there!"

"Cast wouldn't have let us go, not with Tyrellis alive. Even after he stepped away, it took us five more seconds to get out of there. That would have been more than enough time for Cassius to screw up our entire plan. If he had even touched Tyrellis, Nitara would be gone now."

Graham grunted. "I say we leave him there."

"Fuck you!" Briar snapped.

"Excuse me?" Graham flexed. "No one told the fool to do what he did. He tried to play the hero. It was stupid."

"Back off, Graham," Jinn interrupted, but kept his eyes on the body of Tyrellis.

"Who are you to tell me what to do?" Graham was tired of playing nice, and tired of being told what to do.

"We can't fall apart here, guys." Rosie stood and placed her hand on Briar's shoulder. She used her magic to soothe the aching heart of the queen.

"I'm not falling apart," Graham, like a child, shot back.

"We need to work on getting Nitara out of there. I don't think she is going to last much longer." Ardyn wanted to redirect the conversation. "The body is starting to deteriorate." They all watched as the vampire's foot grayed, and then turned to ash. It held its form for a moment before collapsing under the air. The ash fell but never touched the floor, it vanished in the air.

"What the hell did they do to him?" Graham stepped forward, his anger quieted for a moment as he looked on in disbelief and fear. "This isn't right. This isn't natural."

"I don't know, but I can barely feel Nitara in there now. She's fading with him." Jinn kneeled beside the body and tried to reach his wife again. He was met with silence.

"Blood!" Bruto yelled. "Get the damn thing some blood!"

"That's a good idea." Ardyn walked away. "We need to create a sterile room to put him in. Somewhere where we can be sure there is minimal disruption to his body." He tried to create the room himself, but was too weak. Even djinn had to rest between using their magic, but Ardyn had done very little resting. He was weakening, and it showed.

"Here, let me help," Rosie offered. She waved her hand, and the room appeared. Glass walls surrounded a sterile lab with a bed to place the body. With Jinn's help, she carefully moved Tyrellis into the room. During the move, the vampire lost a finger. Again, it vanished into the air.

"How are you going to get the blood into his body? I doubt an I.V. will work." Jinn examined their subject matter.

"His mouth. It's an easy access point. And his head seems to be the better part of his body. Everything else appears to be too fragile, and I doubt a vein would actually accept a needle right now."

"I'll go get something from my supply. I'm sure real blood will work better than anything you conjure up." When the others looked at him with raised brows, Graham responded with sarcasm, "Hell, I'm a vampire, and as much as I love the synthetic stuff, I need the real stuff from time to time."

Within a matter of minutes, Tyrellis was set up in the room with the blood supply pumping into his mouth. They watched closely as signs of life returned to him; the decay slowed and slowly reversed. They increased the intake, but it wouldn't be enough to sustain him for long.

"Briar, can you put a call in to Sybella? Maybe she can help?" Jinn questioned the woman who stood nearby, making her own assessments of the magic at play.

"Um, yeah. I'll try." Her expression was holding something back from the others. Something about the magic felt familiar, but she couldn't put her finger on it. "I'm sure she'll have better luck than I am right now." She nodded to Jinn and she made her exit, careful to avoid the vampire who had gotten under her skin.

"He's burning through that, and he's still not healing. The look of his other foot is getting worse and I'm afraid he may lose that leg, too. This will buy us some time, but not much." Graham watched the decaying vampire closely. "His body isn't absorbing any of the blood. It's burning off just about as fast as we can get it in. I'll make a run for some more. I have a feeling what I have in stock will not be enough." Without further discussion, Graham left the room and headed toward the Hub's exit.

"You're not going to like what she had to say." Briar returned to the sterile room where Jinn remained watching the body. The decay had spread and Tyrellis was short one knee and one hand. "Shit, it's getting worse."

"Yeah, and fast." Jinn took his eyes off of the body. He'd been trying to reach out to Nitara and continued to be met with a heartbreaking silence. "What is it?"

"Well, the short version of it is that you're going to have to jump right on in there and pull Nitara out." Briar frowned.

"What?" Jinn looked back at the body and then back at Briar. "How the hell does she expect me to jump inside of a dying vampire and make it out alive?"

"Well, of course, there will be provisions. She gave us a spell. It's a ritual that we will have to perform the entire time you're on your rescue mission." She paused; her hesitation only made the frown lines in Jinn's forehead deeper. "You'll need a tether, something to keep you linked to us here, or you will get trapped inside."

"Right, a tether." He ran his hands through his hair. "I damn sure am not trying to get stuck in there."

"And it has to be someone who shares Nitara's heart," Briar continued, though he hadn't fully processed what she'd already told him. Might as well get it right out there in the open.

"What?" He looked at her. "What does that mean?"

"It means someone who she loves." Briar paused and stepped back as Ardyn entered the room. "Other than you." Briar looked at Ardyn. "It has to be you."

"You've got to be fucking kidding me." Jinn wanted to scream, punch something, but in the room with the delicate decaying corpse, he couldn't.

"I ..." Ardyn caught the tail end of the conversation enough to understand why Jinn was glaring at him like he wanted to murder him. "I don't know what to say. I had no idea that she—"

"Fuck it, we don't have time to discuss this," Jinn cut him off. He didn't want to hear Ardyn's explanation or lack thereof. It would not help them. "What else did she say? What am I supposed to do?"

"Like I said, she gave us the ritual and instructions on how to properly perform it. My team is already working to get things in order. We should be ready to go in an hour."

"Good, let's get this shit over with." Jinn couldn't take being in the room anymore, even if it meant that she would fade away while he was gone. He had to get out. His mind was cluttered with thoughts of loss and betrayal, nothing that would help him in this situation.

"Jinn." Ardyn exited the Hub to join Jinn out in the fresh air.

"Look, man, not right now." With his back to the approaching man, Jinn held his hand up to stop him. "I know you likely have a lot to say and you feel like you have to get it off your chest right now, but trust me, I don't want to hear it."

"I get that," Ardyn continued, because he was hardheaded and a glutton for punishment. "I just really think that you need to know that nothing like that has ever happened between us. I know what you're thinking, but it's wrong."

"I already told you, I don't need or want to hear what you have to say about this." Jinn turned to him. "We're getting Nitara out of the vampire. I'm getting my friend from your vampire bitch, and then I'm going home."

"I just—"

"Clearly, I won't get any peace here. Tell Briar to call me when she's ready. She knows how to reach me." Jinn vanished in true djinn style, leaving nothing but a few strands of smoke behind.

"Looks like you've really stepped in it." Rosie was standing just beyond the entrance as Ardyn returned. "Sorry, it was kinda hard not to hear, what with me eavesdropping and all."

"I don't even know what to say." Ardyn shook his head. "This isn't what I would have ever expected to hear."

"There's nothing you can say, as Jinn so clearly pointed out." She pushed off the wall to follow his slow trek toward his room. "So, you and Nitara are more than friends. It is what it is."

"That's just it. We're only friends. Nothing more. Never have been." He denied the allegations. "I don't understand what is happening."

"Perhaps, to you, she's just your friend, but maybe she sees you as something more?"

"Trust me, if Nitara felt that way about me, I would have known."

"Would you? In my experience, men have a tendency to be completely unaware in cases like this." She glanced over her shoulder at Bruto, who was talking to a fairy. "A woman can be completely infatuated with a man, for centuries even, and he would never notice."

"Completely infatuated, huh?" He followed her gaze to the man behind them. He—like everyone else—could see there was something that existed between the two, but neither of them would ever tell. It seemed Rosie had just let a bit of the secret slip.

"Well, apparently something is there. The seer said so." She turned the topic back to the matter at hand. Rosie was there to protect her friends, and Ardyn, as sweet as he seemed to be, wasn't one of them. Not yet anyway.

"I don't know what the seer said or what she saw, but trust me, it isn't that. It can't be."

The Hub fell quiet as everyone went to their collective corners. Things were far too tense between Jinn and Ardyn, and no one wanted to risk stepping on any toes. It was best to keep quiet and let everything resolve itself without interference. It was two hours before Briar and the rest of the fairies were ready to perform the ceremony.

"Everyone needs to be present for this. We are going to need to tap into each of your magic to make sure that the cast is strong enough to hold them through this process," Briar instructed the leaders in the group. Omar, a slither who wasn't as humanoid as their leader, stepped up to take Mike's place. He got his people together.

The small space where Tyrellis rested was packed with bodies—all of whom watched as the fairies worked quickly and gently to prepare the body. After laying a mixture of herbs carefully conjured by Rosie over Tyrellis, they then tied Ardyn with bindings made of the same herbs, which would work as the anchor for Jinn and the bridge for Nitara to cross. A thin thread was then tied around both Jinn's and Ardyn's wrist.

"Now we must remove the binding that keeps Nitara locked inside," Briar said with a tense face. "I knew it felt familiar. That is because it is fae magic. Another replication, but this one seems much more like the original. Luckily, Boxi took a lot of lessons from Praia before she left us, so our understanding of their magic is a lot stronger than it once was."

Boxi stepped forward and carefully worked the spell as she was taught. One by one, the locks on the plate across Tyrellis' chest disengaged; the last one released with a sigh before the piece vanished. As soon as the binding was removed, they all sighed, but their relief was short-lived.

"That can't be good." Bruto pointed to the bottom of the vampire's leg, which turned gray and then to ash that disappeared in the air. The spell that was killing Tyrellis sped up the moment they interfered with the magic that kept Nitara locked away.

"We have to hurry," Ardyn urged, and got a look of disdain from Jinn for daring to speak.

"Jinn, it's time," Briar barked. "You go now, or you don't go at all!"

"Yeah, okay, what do I do?"

"You just ... jump in." She shrugged.

"Jump in?" He rolled his eyes. "She couldn't give any more instruction than that?"

"I guess you would do whatever it is you did with any other vessel." Briar looked at Bruto, who laughed. "I thought you would know how this works, considering you're a djinn and all."

"Yeah, right." The problem was, he never voluntarily entered a vessel. No djinn ever did. It was something that was forced on them. "Well, here goes nothing." He dissolved into blue smoke that hovered above Tyrellis' body before it was absorbed into his chest.

Jinn's body materialized in a way that made him feel less than himself. On some level, he felt whole, but not entirely. He hadn't missed the feeling of being trapped inside of something with no control of getting out. How many years had he spent waiting for someone to rub that stupid pot and set him free? He could still feel the string wrapped around his wrist, tying him to the outside world, and it was the only thing that kept him from freaking out entirely. As he moved through the dark void, he called out Nitara's name.

"Nitara, please answer me." His voice echoed back to him, but the sound was distorted, as if the death was enough to take the life out of even a reflection of his voice.

This was different from the vase. It was weird being inside of something that was alive and yet not. He could feel the death as it crept through Tyrellis' body and it was moving fast. He had to find Nitara and get her out. Opening himself to her, he searched for the feeling of the one who held his heart. She was there, fading, just as her captor was.

"Nitara!" he called out, and the essence of her life perked up and sent a small spark to his heart. That was all he needed to continue. "I'm here. I need you to answer me! Let me know where you are, Nitty, please!" Finally, after saying her name three more times, he finally heard a small voice respond to him.

"Jinn?" Nitara sat in a corner, darkened by the surrounding decay. It was taking hold. Her skin was grayed, and her usual aura that once shone with the colors of love and peace had become darkened by its touch.

"We have to get you out of here." Falling to her side, he tried to lift her up, but her body was weighed down, trapped by the floor that grew around her.

"I can't go. He doesn't want me to." She struggled to speak the words.

"He is dying. Nitara, he can't tell you what to do anymore." Jinn stepped back. "I'll be damned if a dead man is going to take you away from me." With a risky move, Jinn concentrated his own magic into a thin blade. He used the sharp blue form to cut her free and pull her away from the darkness. He lifted her into his arms, but her body felt like it weighed a thousand times more than he remembered.

"No, you don't understand. My life is bound to his. I can't leave." She reached up and touched his face softly. No matter how much he wished for it, it wouldn't change the circumstances.

"Yes, you can. Daegal is gone. Tyrellis is dying, and you are not going with him."

"If he doesn't wish me to be free, I can never be." She shed a tear. "You have to get out of here. I can't let you risk everything for me, not again."

"There is no way I'm leaving you. Hell, I came this far, just for you." Holding her tightly, he looked around. "There has to be a way to get you out of here." He tried to use the connection to Ardyn to pull him back, but as long as he held on to her, he couldn't return.

"If you stay, you will die just like I will." Nitara's eyes watered and tears started to flow. "It's bad enough if I'm gone, but I can't be the reason that you lose your life as well."

"Nitara, I need you to try. I need you not to give up. I can feel what this place is doing to you and I need you to be stronger than this. There are so many people counting on you to keep going."

"Jinn." She tried to keep her voice strong, to hide her fear, but she failed. She took solace in the idea that she could spend her last moments with the man that she loved.

"Look, I have gone to hell and back for you, and I will continue to do so because I love you. So, you have to fight, you have to want to be here just as much as I want you to. Just as much as all of those people who are out there waiting for you do."

"You loved me more than I could ever hope for," she sobbed. "I never thought it possible, but I always felt your love even when you weren't there. I could feel it reaching out to me."

"Until the moon leaves the sky for the last time, I will love you, and even when the darkness takes over, my love will still shine for you, Nitty." He kissed her.

"Oh, my god." Nitara sighed beneath his lips.

"What's wrong?"

"It's Tyrellis." The world trembled, and the space around them crumbled. Nitara wrapped her arms around Jinn's neck.

"What is it?" Despite the surrounding chaos, Jinn held on to his wife. The sound of the vampire's death was agonizing, but he wouldn't leave her. If they were going, they would do it together. Finally, together.

CHAPTER 19

Last Wish

On the outside, looking in, Ardyn and the others watched as the body of the vampire quickly decayed. Moments became minutes, turning to far too long, and as they all said internal prayers, they watched as the rest of his body collapsed on itself and left everyone there staring at a pile of ash. A second later, there was nothing. Tyrellis was gone, and so were the two who were trapped inside of him.

"They didn't make it," Briar gasped. "Oh, my god."

Ardyn fell to his knees. "I ... I felt them. They were okay, and then they were just gone."

"No, fix this!" Bruto yelled. "You said this would work!"

"There is nothing we can do. He had to get her out before ..." Briar couldn't say it. They had gone through so much just for them to turn up empty-handed, and not only did they lose Nitara, but they lost Jinn with her.

"Nothing you can do? Your seer saw this working, right? Ask her! Tell her to fix this!" Bessie was the one who yelled, and Bruto held her back.

"Look, we did all we could!" Boxi stood in front of Briar. She would protect her queen if things got out of hand.

"We all did." Briar placed her hand on the empty bed. "Jinn could have gotten out of there at any time. But he chose to stay in there with her. He did all that he could to bring her back. It just wasn't enough."

The room fell silent of every noise except the soft sobs of those who stared at the empty bed, mourning their friends. No one ever considered losing. No one ever thought that Jinn wouldn't succeed. He always came through in the end. Rosie kneeled in the space where Tyrellis' body once lay and mourned the loss of her family.

"You guys really need to cheer up." Jinn's voice boomed from behind them. They all turned around to find Jinn holding an unconscious Nitara in his arms. "I mean, I'm the one who had to climb inside a vampire!"

"What the hell?" Ardyn stood slowly as he looked at the man holding his friend in his arms. He thought she was gone forever, the closest thing he had to family, and yet there she was again.

"How did you get out of there?" Bruto stepped forward and peered down at Nitara, who still held a gray tint to her skin.

"It was the vampire." Jinn gazed down at his love.

"What?" Briar pushed everyone out of the way and ushered Jinn to the bed, where he could lay Nitara's body.

"He wished her free." He shook his head as he watched the woman closely. Even outside of his arms, he could still feel the chill that held on to her. "It was just before everything went dark, or darker."

"He did?" Ardyn asked as he stepped closer to the bed, but paused as Jinn's angry glare found him.

"Yes, Sarah's betrayal. It broke him." Nitara's eyes parted, and she stared up at the man who had yet again saved her life. "It was Jinn's love for me. Somehow, it touched the icy heart of Tyrellis. His last thought before he was gone from my mind was his wish that I be free to experience a love that he never had." She watched him for a moment longer before her eyes slid shut again.

"That's beautiful," Bessie sighed.

"Yeah, well ..." Jinn cleared his throat, "she needs to get rest. Briar, will you make sure she is okay? Do whatever you have to do to make her skin turn back to normal. We need to be sure that she isn't still being affected by whatever the hell they did to that vampire."

"I'll help," Ardyn offered, and Jinn groaned, turned, and left the room.

"How did you get in there without being trapped?" Nitara turned her head on the pillow to look at Jinn. Once they'd gotten her stabilized, he returned to the room and refused to leave until she woke again.

"It's a long story." He shrugged.

"I have time." She lifted her hand, which trembled before it dropped back down to the bed beside her. "Doesn't look like I'll be going anywhere anytime soon."

"I had to be anchored to someone else."

"Someone else?" She looked over his shoulder at the group that was huddled in the area outside of her transparent room.

"Yeah. Look, I need to get out there." He followed her gaze to the others. They were gathering to plan the next part of their rescue mission. "We have to figure out how we're going to get Mike back. We got you out, but now he is trapped in there with the vampires, and we don't know how much longer they are going to keep him alive. You rest up. Okay?"

"Jinn?" she called.

He turned back to her. "Yes?"

"Are you okay?"

"Don't worry about me." Returning to her, he ran the tips of his fingers down her cheek. "Rest. Please." When she smiled, he kissed her forehead and turned to leave the room.

Boxi entered shortly after. She checked Nitara's vitals and smiled. "Soon, you'll be back on your feet. It looks like the fae magic is just about gone. How do you feel?"

"A little shaky, but other than that, I'm okay." Nitara kept her eyes on Jinn, who joined the others outside of the room.

"That is to be expected." Boxi propped up more pillows behind her head.

"Do you know what's going on with him?" Nitara sat up with the fairy's help. "There is something that he isn't telling me, and I can't seem to figure it out or get him to open up to me. I'm used to him getting into his brooding states, and I know with my leaving the way I did, he would be upset, but there is something more to this, something deeper. Do you know what it is?"

"Well, yeah, I think so." The woman considered if she should be the one to reveal the secret to Nitara. It really wasn't her place, but she also knew that Nitara wouldn't give up on her questioning.

"What is it?" Nitara turned to her. "Tell me. He won't, and if he is going to go in there fighting vampires, we need to figure this out now. He needs to work through this, or his head will be clouded, and his judgement skewed."

"Ardyn." Boxi let the name fall from her lips, almost as if it was unintentional.

"Ardyn? What about him?" Nitara scoffed. What could Jinn possibly be so upset about that concerned the hybrid? Did he wish he could turn into a wolf as well?

"The seer told us that there needed to be an anchor in place, something to hold Jinn here and create a bridge for you to cross on your way out. She told us he had to be anchored by someone who holds your heart, someone that you love." Boxi held Nitara's gaze as she searched her eyes for the confirmation. Was there love there? Did Nitara truly feel what the seer said she did for Ardyn?

"Ardyn," Nitara sighed with understanding.

"Yes." The fairy nodded.

She shook her head. "Jinn thinks that means that I'm in love with Ardyn."

"Well, yeah, we all do." Boxi shrugged. "You told him you were leaving for another man. We just assumed that this meant there was some truth to that."

"Okay, I've rested enough. I need to go see him." Nitara struggled to get to her feet. When she was upright, a wave of dizziness rushed her, and she fell back down.

"Maybe you should take more time to rest? There will be plenty of time to clear things up." Nitara watched as Boxi glanced at the man who was focused on the group. "Besides, right now really isn't the time. This seems like a private discussion, one that shouldn't be done in front of the entire group."

"Perhaps you are right." She didn't want to embarrass anyone with her confession. It might make Jinn feel better, but it might also crush Ardyn if he, like everyone else, believed that she was in love with him.

"Yeah, they aren't planning to move until tomorrow night. Please, just take a few more hours to heal. After that, you should be just fine." Boxi smiled as she helped Nitara lay back onto the plush surface. "Don't hesitate to call me if you need anything." She placed a small cube in her hand. "Just whisper into this, and I will hear you."

"Thank you, Boxi." Nitara placed her free hand over the girls. She felt a connection with her, something inexplicable, yet comforting.

"It's my pleasure." She smiled and left Nitara to rest.

"Jinn?" the soft voice called from the doorway to his room and his heart stopped.

"Nitara?" He stood from the corner of the room where he'd set up for his meditation. "What are you doing here? You're supposed to be resting."

"I couldn't rest, not after what I heard."

"What was that?" He ushered her to the bed where she could sit comfortably.

"Boxi told me what's wrong with you, why you're acting so odd." She melted into the mattress, which was much more comfortable than the one they'd had her on. Finally, he stopped fussing over her and sat down beside her on the bed.

"I guess she has just as big of a mouth as her queen. Look, if you have feelings for Ardyn, that's fine. What I said back there, when I was getting you out, it doesn't matter. I didn't say it to make you feel bad or to make you feel in any way obligated to me. As long as you're happy and not in danger, that is all that matters."

"You really do love me way too much, you know that?" She smiled at him. "I swear I don't deserve it."

"Perhaps, but nothing is going to change the way I feel about you. I'm okay with that." He pulled her hand into his own.

"Look, I don't love Ardyn, at least not in that way." She found his eyes and held them with her gaze. "Do you understand that?"

"You don't?" His eyes lit up with the happiness her words brought to him.

"No, he is like a little brother or, in a way, a child. When I met him, he was so new to all of this. You know how Daegal does ... he creates a new project, and if it doesn't pan out the way he intended, he just tosses them to the side. That's exactly how it happened this time. Ardyn was supposed to play a bigger part in everything that went down in the Cascades, and I think that is why nothing worked out the way Daegal had hoped. Well that, and how you came in with the calvary. Daegal couldn't break Ardyn. He couldn't control him, and he couldn't place him in a vessel because of his wolf. So Daegal just cut his losses and dropped Ardyn on the side of the road.

"When I found Ardyn, he was here, and it was after Daegal decided to attach me to Tyrellis. The man was getting all his intel about being a djinn from a vampire! Graham was the only one who knew about Ardyn, and lucky for him, Graham was a good guy and didn't immediately turn him over. I had to step in, though. As much as Graham wanted to help, he knew very little, and Ardyn was a danger to himself and everyone around. I taught him everything about surviving this life. Yes, I love him, but like I love family. Maybe stronger because, for the last few decades, he's been the only other person I could confide in or be close to. But trust me when I say this …," She lifted her hand, steady and true, to touch his face. "My heart belongs to no one bu t you."

"Nitty." He sighed and leaned into her touch. His heart warmed with the reassurance of her hand against his face. She was his, always and forever.

She grabbed the chain that held the moon carved by his hand, which hung around his neck. He removed it from his neck and put it back on hers. "Nitara, you will have my heart for as long as the sun rises to kiss the sky, and for an eternity after it fades." Smiling, he pulled her into his arms. "You are my world."

"Good, don't ever let me go."

"Never." The two kissed, for the first time since they'd been torn apart and made djinn, as free lovers, with nothing stopping them from being together.

"Ouch," Rosie whispered as she approached Ardyn. He'd been on his way to speak to Nitara when he overheard her talking to Jinn in his room. He told himself not to eavesdrop, to just walk away, but he couldn't.

"So, you heard all that, huh?" He moved farther along down the hall to make sure he wasn't heard by the couple inside of the room.

"Yeah, I couldn't help it, with the door open." She shrugged. "Not like they were trying to make it a secret, kind of like how you were, all perched outside of the doorway."

"Yeah, well, I told you she didn't feel that way about me." He continued walking, and Rosie followed him.

"But a part of you wanted her to?" She pushed, and when he paused, she knew she had him. "Admit it, holding that bottled up won't do you any good, trust me."

"Maybe, but it doesn't matter now." He stripped off the jacket he'd been wearing and tossed it on the nearby chair.

"Where are you going?"

"I need to go for a run. There's too many people here. I need to clear my head." Ardyn disappeared through the exit to the Hub.

"Okay, wolfy," she whispered after him.

"What's up with him?" Bruto appeared by her side in true barbaric fashion, with no shirt to cover his full pecs and hard abs. She knew exactly what that meant.

"Nitara," she sighed. "That woman really knows how to fuck with a guy's mind, doesn't she?"

"You're not too bad yourself." Grabbing her, he pulled her into a long embrace and covered her mouth with his.

"Tell me something I don't know!" she growled, and as she ruffled her hands in his thick, red hair, they disappeared in a cloud of smoke.

CHAPTER 20

Save a Slither

"Nice of you to return." Graham nodded at Ardyn, who had spent the entire night and the next day on the run. As the sun fell again and he returned to the Hub, he was careful to miss Sarah's men who were out hunting for them. He left Reverie entirely because he needed to get as far away from the place as he could. When Ardyn returned the next morning, everyone was getting their things together, preparing to go and rescue Mike from Sarah.

"Ardyn, you're back!" Nitara ran up to him but halted short of hugging him when he looked at her with eyes that held sorrow and pain. "Where did you go? I came looking for you."

"I needed to run." He grunted, but then softened as he looked at her. They were still friends, still family. He let Rosie get in his mind and convince him that he wanted more from her than he actually did. That wasn't her fault.

"Well, I want to thank you for everything, for going through so much to save me." Nitara hugged the man. Over her shoulder, he spotted Rosie; still instigating matters, she winked at him.

"Of course, you know how much I care about you. I could never just sit back and let you get taken away like that." He looked around the room. "Apparently, there are a lot of people who feel that way about you. You're truly a loved woman." It was as close as he would get to saying what he wanted. Especially with Jinn standing just a few feet away. It was the first time that the man hadn't looked at him like he wanted to kill him. He wouldn't poke the bear!

"Really, thank you." She followed his gaze. "All of you. I know I've said it so many times in the last twelve hours, but really, I appreciate the sacrifice that each one of you has made for me."

"All right, enough of all this sappy shit. Are we ready to do this or what?" Bruto boasted. Always ready for action, he pounded his chest and got slapped on the arm.

"You really need to calm down," Rosie teased. Then leaned into him and whispered, "Save that for later."

Boxi, who was too close for comfort, overheard the comment and groaned.

"Hell, you know I was pent up for too long. I need that bit of action! Besides, who knows how many more of these blazing glories we'll get to be a part of? We have to savor every moment!"

"I just want to get back to my babies." Rosie pouted. And by babies she meant her island of penguins. The woman had a thing for them, and when the world went crazy, she claimed a home full of them. Bruto loved action, but she was a homebody and her body had been away from home for far too long.

"Yeah, you'll get there soon enough." He winked at her. He would be right there with her, and those annoying ass birds.

"Look, Mike has been by my side for a long time. Even when I didn't want him there. He's also done a lot for everyone in this room, even when it didn't seem to benefit him much." Jinn took hold of the room. "He is one of us! And I will not leave this damn place until he is by my side. We go in there, and we don't leave until we have him! Understood?"

While the others nodded in agreement and pumped themselves up for the fight to come, Graham snuck out the back. Briar, who saw him make his exit, decided to follow.

"Hey, Graham," she called out to him.

"Yes?" He turned to her.

"Where are you going?" she asked, giving him the chance to cop out of his cowardice and return inside.

"Excuse me?" He looked over his shoulder as if she was directing her comment to someone unseen. "Last I checked, I don't answer to you."

"You're coming with us to get Mike, right?" She glanced back at the others, who vanished as the wall solidified and closed them out.

He laughed. "No, I think I'll sit this one out."

"You've got to be kidding me." Briar rolled her eyes at the sad excuse of a man.

"What's your problem?" he huffed as he turned to continue his escape route.

"My problem? What's yours?" He continued to walk away from her, but she kept on his heel. "What the hell problem could you possibly have with Mike? You don't even know him!"

"I know enough about him and his kind to know I want nothing to do with them."

"Is that so?"

"Yeah, that's so." He grunted at her.

"And what is it you know?" Briar wanted to light the vampire's ass on fire, but she held back.

"I know they are weak, cowards, and they will stab you in the back the first chance they get," he growled as his steps became heavy with his growing rage.

"Okay, I get it. Someone hurt you. I'm gonna take a wild guess and say it was a slither. Am I right? Fine. Be mad at *that* person!" she yelled. "Not at Mike. He doesn't deserve that, not after everything he's been through."

"Everyone wants me to think he is some noble hero." He finally stopped walking and turned on his unwanted shadow. "I don't buy it!"

"Think whatever the hell you want, but he is a hero! To a lot of people, that man is exactly that." She paused for a moment before continuing. Yelling at Graham would do nothing but give him more fuel for his ignorance. "Mike is the one who realized what Daegal was up to. He is the one who found Nitara. If it weren't for him, none of us would be here. When it was time to stand against that bastard, I remember your people were called because of your strength, and not a damn one of you answered! Like the rest of the world, you sat back and let us handle it. But Mike and his people were right there by our side. They were fighting to protect not only themselves, but every fucking life on this planet. And you have the nerve to stand there and question his actions?"

"Whatever." Graham didn't have a solid retort, but she could see that he would ignore even the clearest logic.

"Yeah, whatever. Tell me something, vampire. How brave were you? What did you do to try to save *your* people? Tyrellis was here, stirring up shit, running things into the ground. And what did you do? Nothing! I can tell you what Mike did for his people. I can tell you he faced hell itself to make sure that his people's suffering ended. Hell, if you were half the man he is, you'd be lucky." She turned to head back inside the Hub to rejoin the others. "We'll just be out there, saving your people from the bitch that wants to take over. But feel free to step in and claim your victory when the dirty work is done."

This time, when they approached the vampire capital, they went full force. Sarah would be expecting them, and she would have her people in place to be damn sure they would have to fight like hell to make it through their borders. Bruto was at the lead of their charge—the djinn rode down the main street of the town that led right to her door on a cloud of orange smoke. Blasting classical music as he moved through the streets, he used flashes of orange light that temporarily stunned any vampires who tried to attack him along the way. The aim was to subdue, not kill, at the request of Graham. They were still his people, and they didn't deserve to die because their leader was an insane bitch.

The short-term paralysis was enough to give their crew the time they needed to make it to the main event. While Bruto took the focus of their enemy, the others ran for the oversized mansion housing Sarah and their captured friend, Mike. At the gates outside of the structure, they regrouped. Just on the other side were a line of vampires, a mixture of old blood and new blood. The feral look in the eyes of the newborns was the only way to tell between the two. Rosie stood at the head of their collective.

"All right, boys and girls, this is what we came here for!" she called out as she swayed her hips and paced slowly in front of the gate. The vampires hissed from the other side. "They have our friend, and we aren't leaving here without him. Beyond these gates, those who stand against us must suffer the consequences!" The band of heroes cheered her on and she basked in their adulations. "Let's show these damn blood suckers what we can do!" Rosie turned to the gates, held out her hands, and pummeled the enforced bars with her magic. They shook beneath the blow but remained intact. She peered over her shoulder at Ardyn. "Come on, wolfy, give a girl a hand."

Ardyn joined her and together they blasted the gates. The green and pink streams hit with full force, but it looked as though they would fail. Briar landed beside Ardyn, nodded at him with understanding, and added her magic to theirs. They needed more power; the sun was set, and her magic wasn't as strong. She called to Boxi, who used her affinity for earth to shake the ground beneath them. The bars bent and the vampires on the other side prepared for the destruction to come.

With a massive explosion, the frame burst into jagged pieces that went flying into the inside. The shattered bars turned into spears that impaled some of the vampires who charged them and cut down their opposition's numbers instantly. The explosion shattered the windows behind them and shook the foundation of the massive home. Their enemy struggled to recover from the attack, and their lost focus gave the intruders the upper hand. Rosie issued her battle cry, and the group ran forward.

CHAPTER 21

One Sick Bitch

Nitara *pushed through the doors* that barely remained attached to their hinges. Behind her, the battle waged on, and though her side had taken a few casualties, they were winning. At the top of the grand stairs, where Tyrellis once sat, was his sadistic widow, Sarah. She was perched atop his throne, dressed in a long red dress. With her legs crossed, and an expression of pure pleasure on her face, she scented the air and smiled.

"Don't you just love that? The smell of rage!" Sarah gazed down at Nitara, who continued her approach.

"You are one sick bitch, you know that?" Nitara looked around the room where there were fallen vampires; they'd been taken out with the explosion outside.

"People keep telling me that." She sighed. "Smart, yes! Calculating, oh yeah! Innovative, check mark! But sick? No, I am not sick. I saw an opportunity, and I took it!"

"You killed him!" Nitara screamed.

"Oh, look, I think you got a case of Stockholm syndrome." Sarah laughed. "Did you love him? Will you miss the little twit ordering you around?" She stood from her seat. "A better question still. How the hell are you alive?"

"Nitara!" Jinn entered the doors, catching up with her.

"Oh, isn't this just lovely? How sweet that you all came back for your little friend." Sarah clapped. "I'm assuming that is why you're here, right? This is another one of your pathetic rescue missions. Don't you people ever get tired?"

"You bitch," Inda spat as she landed through the shattered window. "Where is he?!"

"Oh goodie! It's the fire bird! You, I particularly enjoy." She tapped her foot on the step beneath her. "Too bad our last encounter was cut short."

"If you want a repeat, just pucker up and kiss my flaming ass!" Inda smirked, commenting on burns that still hadn't healed on her hands, and the ones masterfully covered with makeup on her face and chest. The fire of a phoenix differed from anything on Earth, and the vampires who encountered it often never healed completely.

"No need to be disgusting," Sarah snipped. "You can have your friend. Take him and go."

"Yeah, right, what's the catch?" Jinn asked. "Why would you hand him over so easily? What do you want?"

"Smart man! Fine, what I want is simple. Nitara stays here. Or whichever one of you wish-granting beings who want to fall on the sword. You're all so self-sacrificing. Really, I don't care which one of you do it."

"You're crazy if you think that's going to happen." Jinn pushed himself forward. "No one is staying here with you."

"She," her crimson-painted nail pointed to Nitara, "belonged to my husband, and upon his death, all of his belongings transferred to me. But you stole her from me, so that means I'm owed a djinn. Anyone will do." She held up a silver bracelet. "Just climb the stairs and put this on. It's kinda like that binding thing you had going on with Tyrellis, only this one was crafted for me."

"You think either of us will just offer to do that?"

"Yes, as a matter of fact, I do." From the balcony above, they could hear chains rattling. Within a moment, he came into view. Mike was bound by barbed shackles that dug into his flesh. Sarah pointed at one of the vampires who pulled on the chains. They tightened, and Mike screamed as they cut deeper into his flesh. "I don't think he's going to last much longer."

"Mike!" Jinn called out and leaped onto the balcony above. The vampires who guarded him attacked, but before they could land one blow, they all fell to the floor wrapped in strings of blue flame that burned their flesh. Their screams quickly ended with their deaths. Mike leaned against the banister, tired from the torture they subjected him to.

"I wouldn't touch those chains if I were you," Sarah warned, but Jinn ignored her.

The moment Jinn's hand touched the chains, he felt an intense burning sensation as his flesh was seared. "Fuck!" he yelled as he pulled his hand back.

"Well, I warned you." Sarah laughed as she began to descend the stairs. "Like I said, I am a calculating bitch. I saw an opportunity to make a few allies when all the world was focused on the shit happening in dragon land. There were a few, those who were afraid of what would happen to them if he succeeded. They were looking for a safe place to stay and I offered that to them. Well, wouldn't you know it? That put them in my debt?"

From outside, Briar ran in. "*Fae!*" she yelled, and through the window, they could see Sarah's unexpected allies. "The others can't get in. I barely made it. They've reinforced the barrier!"

"Well, now you've gone and ruined my grand reveal!" She stopped in the middle of the staircase. "Oh, but no matter. I have fae on my side, which means you will do as I say, or you will all die!"

"I have to say, you really surprised me," Nitara spoke as she approached Sarah.

"Is that so?" The woman was nervous now, and Nitara could hear it in the way her voice trembled. Even with having the upper hand, Sarah wasn't as confident as she wanted them to believe.

"I never suspected you." Nitara stepped forward. "All this time, I never thought you were the kind to betray him. I was so busy looking outside of the home that I didn't realize the biggest threat was living inside its walls. I guess you fooled us both that way."

"Yes, well, now you know. I don't have all day here. Are you going to step up and save your friend or not?" She held out the bracelet, dangling it from the tip of her finger.

"No, she isn't." Jinn leaped from the balcony above and landed between the two of them.

"And you aren't either." Nitara pushed him back. She was done being saved by him and everyone else. This was her fight.

"Mike is my friend, and you've been through enough with this shit." He looked back up to where he left his friend. "Besides, I owe him. If it weren't for him, you wouldn't be here now."

"Look, I don't care who does it." Sarah sighed. "A djinn is a djinn." Just as she took another step toward them, a fae girl emerged on the balcony with Mike. "Oh look, and now I have him again!"

Mike's body went flying over the edge of the balcony and the chain binding him to the ceiling. With a sharp jolt, the line snapped and left Mike's body dangling in the air above them. He screamed from the impact for a moment before the searing pain knocked him unconscious. Through the front and side doors, a combination of fae and vampire filed into the room.

"Isn't this just delicious? Yeah, apparently there's a little bad among all of us." She smiled. "You try anything, and they will make sure none of you leave here alive. I wonder how long you'll last. Already, one of your team members here is weaker than you'd want me to believe. Your fairy queen is all but useless with the moon hanging above us!"

"You will never get what you want!" Nitara spat at the vampire.

"Oh, but it seems I will." Smiling, she held out the spelled bracelet once again. "Now, who's it gonna be?"

Nitara looked over her shoulder at Jinn and they made brief eye contact. That was all that they needed to have complete understanding of how things would go down. Their connection was just as strong as it ever was. They needed to buy time. The slithers who had taken a back entrance were nearly in place. Ardyn confirmed it with the green flash of light that displayed outside of the window. They needed only a few more minutes before they could strike. Nitara slowly nodded to Jinn. His eyes flickered to Mike and back. That was the cue.

Things were going to move fast. With the moon in the sky, Sarah had the upper hand. She was right about the fairies; they weren't as strong, but they were still a contender. Besides, they had a lot more firepower on their side. Bruto had done more scouting and the orange flare on the opposite side of the building was their confirmation that Sarah had pulled all of her aces.

Jinn, with eyes trained on Mike above, walked closer to Sarah, who remained on the steps. She kept a brave face, but the slight tremble at her fingertips betrayed the poker face she attempted to hold. She was anxious, and that energy would play against her.

"Well, I guess we have our volunteer." She smiled.

"Just get it over with!" Jinn snapped.

Sarah, happy to comply, descended the rest of the stairs and stood in front of Jinn. She opened the bracelet and grinned victoriously as she reached for his outstretched hand. Just as she was about to snap it into place, Nitara cracked her whip and the tip of it smacked the bracelet out of Sarah's hand. The spelled piece went flying across the room where the fae and vampire ran for it. Their distraction was the perfect moment for the slithers to jump into action. The doors burst open and one by one, reptilian forms filled the room. They wasted no time in their attack, but the fight was a struggle because the fae were still strong.

"You will never win this fight!" Sarah cried out. "You will be mine!"

"Okay, you have fae on your side. We have fairies, dragons, and djinn!" Inda was fed up. "Fuck this! You want to fight, bring it!" She turned around and dove through the window she entered. Outside she took to the sky, dodging the magical shot sent from the ground, and found Jax. "They have Fae, you know what that means!" With understanding, Jax and the dragons who joined him turned their flame towards the sky. While their flames lit the heavens, the ice dragons joined. The combined forces created a cloud of smoke so thick that it blocked the moon from the fae below. Weakened by their disconnection from the source of their power, the fae retreated.

"What the fuck? *Fight*!" Sarah yelled, but her allies knew they were at a disadvantage and, one by one, they fled the scene.

Outside, the barrier that kept the others at bay faltered and Bruto and Rosie pounced on the opportunity. Their magic combined was strong enough to overpower what was left, and once again, the battle outside was on. Jax and the other vampires took to setting flame to the parameters around the compound to avoid any other vampires joining the battle inside. Inda added her flame to the mix as well, knowing the damage caused would be enough to deter anyone who dared to try to cross it.

"You've been beat, Sarah. Just give it up!"

"No! I haven't!" Her eyes scanned the room and for a moment, she looked panicked until she realized Mike was still hanging above. She pointed to him and shouted, "Mike! He is still mine and none of you will be able to get him without me! That is spelled against all of you! Only a vampire can save him, and it appears you're without one!"

"Dammit, Graham," Briar muttered. He was the only one they had on their side, but the man was too stubborn to get over himself to come help them.

"You rang?" The vampire appeared in the window behind them. "I figured I would let you all work out your shit before I joined the party."

"Oh, how nice of you." Briar rolled her eyes.

"You mean to tell me, a vampire can snatch those chains off of our buddy up there? Great!" Smiling, Graham made a dash for Mike, but his body slammed against the wall when Sarah attacked.

"No! You will not take this from me!" she screamed, punching him over and over in the face, nearly knocking him unconscious before a stream of fire blasted her side and sent her flying off of him and onto the floor.

"Fuck!" Graham patted his thigh, that was caught in the flame.

"My bad. My aim is a little off." Inda shrugged, but winked at Briar.

"I saw that!" Graham grunted. "You did that on purpose!"

"Yeah, well, maybe next time you will get your head out of your ass!" She pointed to the man who was still dangling above them. "Get him, now, please."

Graham jumped to the ceiling and unhooked the chain, and Mike's body slammed into the floor beneath. Jumping down, he landed on the ground beside him. "Done."

"You're such an asshole!" Inda spoke. "Get the chains off of him!"

They all surrounded Mike as the chains were removed from his body. When the last one was off, Graham tossed them into a corner, away from the group. Mike gasped as his lungs filled with air and his expanding flesh burned where the chains had dug into him.

"Mike, you okay?" Jinn stood looking on at his friend, who slowly came back to consciousness.

"Yeah, I'm good," he lied. The man was clearly in a lot of pain.

"Great, let's get you out of here!" Briar spoke and reached down to help him up.

As they all began to regroup, no one kept an eye on Sarah. She took that as her chance. With Jinn's back toward her, she retrieved the bracelet which had fallen just a few feet from where she landed after the blast and slapped it around his wrist.

"Ha!" she cried out. "You are mine!"

Jinn looked down at his wrist where the bracelet glowed as it activated their connection, and then at Nitara. He could already hear her thoughts. "Nitty, get out of here!"

"No. What are you talking about?" It took Nitara a second too long to realize just how the tables had turned.

"Jinn," Sarah called out with a sick tone to her voice, "kill Nitara!"

The moment the order was issued, the blade of fire appeared in his hand and he charged the woman he'd come there to protect. Nitara was quick on her feet; two whips shot out and wrapped around his ankles and pulled his legs from underneath him. "Jinn, stop!" Nitara screamed, but already he had recovered and was after her again.

"You know I can't," he growled as he turned his blade into a whip that matched hers. He snapped it at her but missed.

Better skilled with her weapon, Nitara dodged his blow while landing one of her own on his right arm. It tore through the leather jacket he wore and ripped through the flesh.

"Fuck!" he screamed, grabbing at the stinging wound.

"You need to fight her!" Nitara demanded from Jinn. "You need to be stronger than this!"

The others had Sarah cornered and just as they were about to grab her, she picked up the enchanted chain and that became her weapon. She smacked Inda in the face with it, knocking her unconscious before she turned her attention to Briar. She wasn't alone. From the balcony above, a few of her minions returned and jumped to the floor beneath, positioning themselves between her and the enemy.

"The cover above is fading!" Bruto entered the room again and took into account everything that was happening. Jinn and Nitara were fighting while the others tried to get to Sarah. "What the fuck is going on?"

"Get Sarah!" Briar yelled. "She has Jinn under her control."

Briar grabbed Inda and dragged her limp body outside. She needed to get her to Jax.

"You will never win! Jinn is mine, and as long as he is wearing that bracelet, he belongs to me!"

"Nitara!" Bruto called as he ran to help her fend off Jinn. "What's the plan?"

"Keep him busy?" Nitara asked and trained her look on Sarah. Around her neck hung a gold chain with strange markings. It was one that Nitara had never seen her wear before. She looked at the bracelet on Jinn's wrist and noticed the design was the same.

"I'll do my best." Bruto grunted as he moved between her and Jinn.

"You're going to have to do better than that." Nitara faded from his side and Jinn tried to find her, but Bruto was quick with his distraction. Streams of orange sprouted from the ground and wrapped around Jinn's limbs. The more he struggled, the more appeared. "Rosie, I need you!" Bruto called out, and as soon as her name passed his lips, she appeared by his side.

"Oh my god, Jinn," she sighed.

"We have to keep him restrained." Bruto grunted as he struggled to hold the man back.

"Right." With no further question, Rosie's pink magic joined Bruto's orange to reinforce the restraints. After the last time Jinn had been turned against them, they'd devised a plan to ensure that they could avoid another disaster.

Across the room, Nitara reappeared between her team and Sarah's. With one strike of her whip, she ended the lives of every vampire who stood between her and Sarah. "Everyone, out," she ordered, and the rest of the team left. All that remained were Nitara, Sarah, and the other djinn. "Tell me something. How did you see this playing out?" She stalked Sarah. "After all that you've heard of us, did you really think that we would give you what you want? Did you think we would just walk away from here and leave one of our own behind?"

"You don't have a choice now! Jinn is mine, and he will be, forever!" Sarah's voice was tense, even she didn't believe her own words. She searched for Jinn, and her eyes displayed her disbelief as she found him restrained by his friends.

"You know, that's what Tyrellis thought. He thought I belonged to him forever. And yet, here I am, and where is he?"

"You're welcome for that," Sarah snapped. "You think you'd be grateful for your freedom!"

"And now you think that you're in any better position than he was?"

"Yes, because, unlike him, I'm not a moron. And I know you won't do anything to me as long as I possess your mate!" Sarah pointed to Jinn, who was still out of commission. "Not that he is doing me much good right now!"

"Here's the thing." Nitara got closer to Sarah, who clutched the spelled chain, her only form of protection, in her hand. "I know your secret."

"What are you talking about?" She backed away as far as she could."

"Jinn's life isn't tied to yours, is it?" Nitara asked, but she knew the answer already.

"Yes, it is!" Sarah searched for a way out but could find no exit that didn't end in her death.

"No, it isn't. The only person with that kind of magic is long gone. You're smart, as you said, so you know that already, don't you?"

"It's too late! I already have him." Sarah's shrill cry echoed around them. "He is mine, and there is nothing you can do about it."

"You have him, for now." Nitara used her whip to take the chain from Sarah; it clattered to the floor and Sarah backed up against the wall. Nitara closed in on the vampire, who was officially all alone. There was no one else to come running in to save her. Nitara kicked aside the head of a vampire she'd taken out. When there were only a few inches left between them, she continued. "Jinn is not yours. He's mine."

"Jinn!" Sarah screamed at the bound Jinn, who failed to kill the woman who held her pinned against the wall. She brought her eyes back to the angry woman in front of her. "Please, don't."

"I'm sorry, are you begging?" Nitara smiled. "It's too late for that!"

"Nitara, what are you doing?" Bruto questioned. They were struggling to hold Jinn back, and Nitara was playing games with the enemy.

"Whatever it is, you might want to get on with it," Rosie shouted. "We won't be able to hold him forever."

"With pleasure." Nitara dissolved into a cloud of purple smoke that hovered in front of Sarah before it shot up her nose and into her mouth.

"No!" Sarah clawed at her face. "Get out!" she screamed. And inside of her head, she heard Nitara's voice. *Your wish is my command.* Sarah's skin turned red with the heat that built beneath her flesh. "Stop!" she cried as her skin began to crack and purple tinted light shone from beneath. It was too late. A moment later, Sarah's body exploded and, in her place, stood Nitara, the chain that bound Sarah to her mate hanging around her neck.

"You can let him go now." She nodded to Bruto and Rosie, who cautiously released their reins on Jinn.

He stood from the floor and watched his wife, who approached him. He gasped as the air forced its way inside his lungs and the sting of his friend's magic diminished. "You're amazing."

"Yeah, I know." Nitara smiled as he took her into his arms.

"Maybe we give these two a bit of privacy and go help the others?" Rosie touched Bruto's arm, and they both vanished from the room.

"How did you know that would work?" Jinn kept his hold around her.

"I didn't. Hell, for all I knew, it would have trapped me right along with you." Reaching up, she took the necklace off and the bracelet dropped from his wrist. Nitara held them both in her hand and the pieces went up in flames. The enchanted metal melted and dripped to the floor. "As I see it, you've already done that, and so much more for me. There was no way I was going to walk out of here and let her have you, not without a fight. I owe you that much."

"You don't owe me a damn thing." Jinn lifted her into his arms and kissed her with a century of passion. "Finally, we can put this shit behind us."

CHAPTER 22

More to do.

"At last, he is awake." Nitara dabbed Jinn's head with a damp towel. "You had me worried there for a bit."

"What happened?" He sat up in the bed and his head spun.

"Oh, you know ... big, bad vampire tried to start some shit, and I saved the day." She gave herself a pat on the back and winked at him.

"Oh, did you?" He laughed. "I vaguely remember that."

"Well, that's the short version." Smiling, she leaned forward and kissed his lips. "I've been waiting to do that."

"Have you?" He lifted his hand to tuck a stray hair behind her ear.

"For far too long." She held his hand against her face and sighed into his touch.

"You should do it again."

Nitara did, and she let the kiss linger before she pulled away once more.

"When did we get back here?" Jinn finally noticed the familiar setting that surrounded them. The last time they were there together, Nitara was in bed and he was nursing her back to health. Things didn't end well that time around.

"Last night. After everything went down, you passed out. Pretty sure it had something to do with that bracelet Sarah slapped on you. I grabbed you and thought of home. I guess since I don't feel like I have one, it brought us to your house even though I intended to go back to the Hub with the others. Once we were here, I didn't want to move you. It seemed a better idea to just wait until you woke up."

"What about Mike?" Jinn repositioned himself. "Is he okay?"

"He is safe and sound. We got him out in time." She poured Jinn a glass of water and handed it to him. "Drink."

"Thanks." He took the offered glass and emptied it of its contents before asking for a refill.

"I called back there; everyone is okay. Briar and the fairies are working on Mike. He will be brought home soon, but they had to intervene to speed up his healing a bit. Graham and Ardyn are leading the cleanup. Reverie will take a while to repair from this. The fae who helped Sarah were rounded up when the sun rose. Boxi and a few other fairies are escorting them home to face the music for their actions. Graham is in for a lot of shit from the fae about what happened."

"So, Graham is taking over?" Jinn finally found a comfortable position on the bed with a pillow tucked behind his head.

"Yeah, he is, with Ardyn by his side." Nitara couldn't help the sense of pride she felt. Ardyn would be sure to keep the vamps on the right path.

"What?" Jinn didn't sound as convinced that it was a good idea.

"Yes, I think it's good. Grahm wants to show the world that vampires aren't that bad." They shared a look, then laughed simultaneously. "Yeah, I know it sounds insane, but he sees how things have started to turn around for Mike and his people. He wants the same for the vampires. Apparently, something Briar said to him really struck a nerve."

"Good luck with that!" Jinn couldn't help the laughter that continued to pour from him. "All I know is that not one blood sucker better come asking me for help with that cause!"

"Oh, you wouldn't lay your life down for them?" She teased him playfully.

"There's only one person in the world that I would do that for." He pulled her into the bed with him and she curled up beside him.

"And who is that?" She kissed his neck.

"Mike, of course!" he joked, and she softly jabbed him in the side. "I kid, I kid!"

"Yeah, you better be!"

The newly reunited couple shared the day together, talking about things that happened while they were apart. Nitara had been through so much, a lot, that was hard for Jinn to hear, but he wanted to know everything. They had missed out on too much time together. Nitara kept assuring him she wouldn't be going anywhere, and they would have all the time in the world to catch up on things, but that wasn't enough for him.

They were curled up together on the sofa and sipping tea. Nitara loved a good spiced chai and Jinn was fond of it as well, but with the addition of a shot of whiskey. She'd just been laughing at him for the modification when their cozy evening was interrupted by a stern knock on the door. Jinn groaned and climbed from the couch where Nitara was lying on his chest.

"Don't move, I'll be right back," he told her as he went to the door muttering about how he wished everyone was still too afraid to come to his door. "What is it?" He swung the door open.

"We've got a problem." The prince of dragons barged into the room with his firebird girl right behind him.

"I see you two have made up." Jinn sighed as he closed the door and followed them to the living room, where Nitara waited.

"What's wrong?" Nitara sat up on the couch and pulled the nearby blanket over her exposed legs. She'd been in nothing but a tank top and panties.

"Rick, he went after the fae girl." Jax said and averted his eyes from Nitara.

"What?" Jinn asked, and Jax turned back to him.

"He overheard me talking about what Mike said about her showing up in shifter land. Next thing I know, I'm getting reports that he is headed that way." Jax spotted the open bottle of whiskey and took a shot straight from it. "We were trying to figure out how to handle this without Mike."

"Without Mike? What's wrong with Mike?" Nitara stood. "Ardyn said he was recovering."

"He is, but he is still pretty messed up. Bruto took him home to rest. He isn't going to be up to any real action for a while," Inda informed them. "Mike said he would send someone in to help us, someone that Jinn trusted. Of course, we never got so far as an introduction to said person, since Rick decided to go rogue."

"And I take it that means our timeline just moved up?" Jinn groaned. "Would it be so terrible to get one day of peace?"

"Yeah, it moved up to yesterday." A frustrated Jax took another shot. "You got anything to eat around here? We need to load up." He looked at Inda, who rubbed her growling belly.

"Food's in the kitchen," Jinn replied, and Inda headed in that direction.

"Do you know where he is?" Nitara stood up, and the blanket was replaced with pants, which made both her and Jax more comfortable.

"Not exactly, but there have been reports of a dragon nearing shifter territory, so we don't have much time. He's one of our fastest guys. I already have a few men trying to cut him off at the pass."

"We need to stop him." Jinn said what they were all thinking. "The shifters will not be pleased if you don't."

"Yeah, if he gets there and starts some shit ..." Jax trailed off.

"It could mean another war." Jinn finished the thought.

"Well, that was a great vacation while it lasted." Nitara sighed and headed toward the kitchen.

"Where are you going?" Jinn called after her.

"Hell, the firebird isn't the only one who needs to fuel up!" She winked at him and laughed as she left the room.

"We really have our hands full, don't we?" Jax chuckled and handed the whiskey bottle to Jinn.

"Yeah, we sure do." Jinn took a swallow of the liquor before they joined the women in the kitchen.

Acknowledgements

I'd like to acknowledge the women who motivated me daily to continue doing what I love. Your encouragement and constant example of the magic we can produce is everything to me! Without you, I don't know how far I would have gotten.

We all need a circle of friends, a tribe who pushes us forward. I'm so lucky to have found mine.

CHAPTER 23

Please Leave a Review

Reviews are the most powerful tools in my arsenal when it comes to getting attention for my books. Much as I'd like to, I don't have the financial muscle of a New York publisher. I can't take-out full-page ads in the newspaper or put posters on the subway.

(Not yet, anyway).

But I do have something much more powerful and effective than that, and it's something that those publishers would kill to get their hands on.

A committed and loyal bunch of readers.

Honest reviews of my books help bring them to the attention of other readers.

If you've enjoyed this book, I would be very grateful if you could spend just five minutes leaving a review (it can be as short as you like) on the book's Amazon page.

Click to Review.

ABOUT THE AUTHOR

Jessica Cage is an International Award Winning and USA Today Bestselling Author of speculative fiction and urban fantasy novels. Publishing since 2010, Jessica made a name for herself in Indie publishing through consistent efforts and organic growth of her platform. The author of 40 fiction novels and 18 short stories published in different anthologies, she continues to produce stories that give representation to marginalized communities in fantasy landscapes.